Cordially Yours, Brother Cadfael

Cordially Yours, Brother Cadfael

edited by

Anne K. Kaler

Bowling Green State University Popular Press
Bowling Green, OH 43403

Copyright 1998 © Bowling Green State University Popular Press

Library of Congress Cataloging-in-Publication Data

Cordially yours, Brother Cadfael / edited by Anne K. Kaler.
     p.   cm.
    Includes bibliographical references (p.   ).
    ISBN 0-87972-773-X (clothbound). -- ISBN 0-87972-774-8
(pbk.)
    1. Peters, Ellis, 1913- --Characters--Brother Cadfael.
2. Detective and mystery stories, English--History and criticism.
3. Monastic and religious life--England--Shrewsbury--History--
Middle Ages, 600-1500--Historiography. 4. Great Britain--
History--Stephen, 1135-1154--Historiography. 5. Historical
fiction, English--History and criticism. 6. Cadfael, Brother
(Fictitious character). 7. Shrewsbury (England)--In literature.
8. Middle Ages in literature. 9. Monks in literature. I.
Kaler, Anne K.
PR6031.A49Z6 1998
823'.912--dc21 .   98-22251
                                     CIP

Cover design by Dumm Art

Contents

The Brother Cadfael Chronicles

Introduction

Anne K. Kaler

Cloying as Brother Cadfael's cordials and just as sweet, Ellis Peters's tales of the twelfth-century Benedictine Abbey of Saint Peter and Saint Paul in Shrewsbury are inscribed in her saga of her soldier-turned-monk, *The Chronicles of Brother Cadfael*. As varied as the herbs hanging from the ceiling of Brother Cadfael's workshop, some of these tales are as bitter as his potions, some as deadly as his elixirs, some as powerful as his soporifics, some as soothing as his balms, some as potent as his purgatives. But, as enjoyable mysteries, these tales are as restorative as Brother Cadfael's own cordials.

Ellis Peters is no stranger to distant days or distant lands in her writings. Under her real name of Edith Pargeter, she wrote a score of other historical novels, including *The Heaven Tree* trilogy, the *Brothers of Gwynedd* novels, and *The Bloody Field*, which also center on an earlier time and an unfamiliar landscape of the Welsh border. Her translations of Czechoslovak literature, her familiarity with India which appears in several of the Felse family detective novels, and her regular mystery novels endeared her to the reading public. Although the bulk of her work still awaits well-deserved scholarly appraisal, Peters's creation of Brother Cadfael and his world has so enchanted the modern reading public and so entranced the viewing public through the filmed versions that the world of academic scholarship would be amiss to neglect *The Chronicles of Brother Cadfael* any longer. This book, then, attempts to fill that need by presenting a series of essays on the appreciation of Peters's talents in creating Brother Cadfael and his world, especially in her ability in weaving the two aspects of mystery and ministry into an enjoyable whole.

In these twenty-one tales—twenty novels and one book of short stories—of the twelfth-century monk, the modern reader is treated to more than a mystery wrapped in a monk's hood. If a monastery seems an unlikely place to shelter murder, mystery, and mayhem, enough of all three regularly creep over those cloister walls to supply Brother Cadfael with puzzles for the *Chronicles*. Yet, within Brother Cadfael's simpler world, Peters creates a tight, lean mystery encased within a multi-layered and regimented world of medieval monasticism. To achieve such artistic asceticism, Peters contrasts the vibrant tapestries of medieval life against the coarse homespun of Cadfael's enviable monastic sparseness.

In doing so, the author cleverly links a curious mind of a scientist/pharmacist with the figure of a knight-errant in her soldier-sailor-monk to form a detective who appeals to the present generation of mystery readers. And what better person for this task than a man dedicated to God, a man whose self-denial clarifies his intellect and whose compassion extends to understanding the workings of God in every human heart. Where the world often forgets that Mercy can suffice when Justice fails, Brother Cadfael never does. Justice may bring the murderer to his deserved end but Mercy escorts his soul before the face of God. In his role as detective uncovering the truth, Brother Cadfael restores Justice to a wronged community: as a member of an order of religious men, Brother Cadfael also serves as Mercy's strongest advocate for the individual soul. It is this delicate balance between world and cloister, justice and mercy, flesh and spirit, man and God that makes Brother Cadfael so appealing in his quest after the "mystery" in the truest sense of that word.

Mystery devotees should not be surprised that detective fiction ultimately imitates man's spiritual search to explain the greatest "mystery" of all—the relationship between God and man. Judging by the increasing numbers of "religious" detectives, modern writers also perceive just how close a "minister" is to a "mystery." Derived from the Greek root meaning closed eyes and lips, the word "mystery" itself has, as its initial meaning, a theological secret while its second meaning indicates its origin from the Latin *ministerium* or work, occupation, ministry, calling, trade, art, or craft. Thus, in medieval times, the word "mystery" also indicated an occupation or service (as in "to minister to") because only a competent craftsperson could know the secret skills of his or her craft. For example, Shakespeare's Othello assumes that Emilia knows her alleged trade as a bawd when he calls upon her to perform "some of your function, mistress . . . Your mystery, your mystery!" by standing watch at her prostitute's door (IV.ii.33, 36). In drama, the medieval French theater developed their *mystere* plays about the miracles or works of Christ and His saints because such performances tried to explain the workings of God's plan in a human universe; in the same manner, the English miracle-play cycles called "mystery" plays were proudly staged by individual craft guilds.

This fine line between "mystery" and "ministry" began to blur until the word took on its modern sense of a "mystery" or a secret knot to be untied by the initiates alone. In contrast, a modern action hero-detective cuts through the mystery with brute strength such as that which Alexander the Great used in hacking the Gordian knot to bits rather than untying it. As the ultimate problem-solver, the detective must unite his logical reason, working on the given information or clues, assemble the clues into a recognizable pattern, and come to the only possible conclusion. Although the process which any detective experiences in untying a mystery follows a set pattern, it is often his ministry or craft of understanding human nature which allows his human compassion to unravel the knotted lives he meets.

If unraveling the knot becomes the detective's quest, then he assumes the role of the knight-errant, one who wanders in search of good deeds and great acts of heroism. The lonely knight is an aberrant force, a "loose cannon" of sorts, one who obeys a higher law than the law itself; in Cadfael's case, he frequently obeys his own internal law of conscience rather than the Higher Law, or its legalistic dictates. Employing Cadfael's common sense as a touchstone, Peters adds the dimension and strictures of a religious setting for her detective. Cadfael could easily have been a townsman, or tradesman, or university don without the complication of a religious affiliation. But the author chooses to have him work within a particular religious framework, namely that of the Rule of Benedict.

In all ages and cultures, religious asceticism calls young men to leave the world to seek the presence of God in the solitude of the wilderness. Although Christian ermeticism lauded solitary saints and desert fathers like Anthony of Egypt, other hermits gathered in loosely formed groups for mutual protection and benefit, their cells replacing the caves, communal prayer replacing individual prayer. Such a person was the sixth-century Benedict of Nursia in Umbria. Having fled his comfortable home and his studies in Rome, young Benedict became a hermit and ascetic whose piety and way of life attracted so many followers that he needed to provide a structure for them to follow. Although Benedict himself preferred a voluntary lay community on the fringe of society rather than an organized monastery, he was prompted to compose a Rule of Life flexible enough to transform separate hermetical experiences into monasticism. The synergy of monasticism became a major civilizing force so that, some six centuries later, Cadfael's choice of the Benedictine monastery was a natural one for a weary wandering soldier seeking stability and order in a disordered world.

Referring to his order as a school in which men learn to serve God, Benedict wisely provided for the separate components of human nature: physical activity, mental stimulation, and spiritual duties. The Benedictine motto, *orare et laborare*—to pray and to work—blended the best of community life with the best of the individual prayer. It stressed the need for physical work and exercise for a healthy body along with two kinds of prayer—community and individual—for a healthy soul. The document advocates a set pattern of silence, solitude, prayer, humility, and obedience. Thus, Peters shows Cadfael's personal charisma as being nicely balanced between worldly experience and the Benedictine way of life—the balanced blend of manual labor, sacred reading, and prayer. The Benedictine abbey gives Cadfael the safe haven from which to unravel the mysteries in *The Chronicles* along with a system of checks and balances to monitor his particular pursuit of justice.

The Benedictine Rule suggests that, when manual labor is dedicated to God, it not only strengthens the body but also provides time for private silent prayer. Benedict, scholars assure us, was the first to raise manual work from the demeaning level of that done by slaves to a position so sanctified that even the tools used in manual work must be considered as sacred as the vessels of the altar. Just how internalized this precept has become in Cadfael appears in his annoyance when his apprentices break his containers or a malefactor breaks a moral or civil law. The second discipline Benedict suggests is that of intellectual stimulation in the required reading of the Scriptures and other sacred writings (*lectio divina*), which also involved memorization, reading aloud, and meditation. If Peters chooses to have Cadfael's study of medieval pharmacology substitute for the *scriptorium*, it is the reader who profits from the lush detailing of Cadfael's natural world.

The third and most important division of the Benedictine's life is the community praying of the Divine Office, that lengthy recitation of set liturgical prayers said in choir with the other monks. Such a recitation of the Divine Office (*opus dei*) encourages physical activity involved in the changing positions of the act of chanting, intellectual challenge in following the intricate musical rhythms, and an emotional outlet in performing the familiar stories and songs of the faith. So ingrained is this rhythm of the Hours that Cadfael continues to practice it even when he has broken his vows of obedience and of stability in not returning to the monastery in *Brother Cadfael's Penance*. And, if a Higher Power occasionally provides the solution to the mystery, who is Cadfael to quibble?

In practice, the Benedictine motto reduces the three actions to a simpler dichotomy—to pray and to work. Thus, for Brother Cadfael, the Benedictine Rule by which he lives seems more equally divided between the recitation of the Divine Hours in the company of his troublesome and troubled confreres and the more peaceful manual labor of preserving his medicinal herbs in his beloved workshop. Even though Brother Cadfael's balance seems to teeter between the civil justice represented by Hugh Beringar and the compassionate mercy of Abbots Heribert and Radulfus, Peters brings all aspects of the Benedictine Rule into play to maintain her character's precarious position as monk and man, father and friend, physician and psychologist, human and humanitarian.

That same sense of balance between seeming paradoxes is what this book attempts to achieve in the essays on the "mystery" of Brother Cadfael's religious values and the "ministry" of his physical crafts. In an interview with Sue Feder, Edith Pargeter/Ellis Peters herself admits that "the writing of these books [*The Chronicles of Brother Cadfael*] has given me more pure pleasure than anything else I have done. . . . There is a foreground and a background, in both of which sacred and secular move in counterbalance."[1] The emphasis within the book moves from essays on the sacred values to essays on the secular crafts and abilities which Cadfael employs in investigating the mysteries.

The first part of the book centers on the mysteries of Cadfael, specifically detailing Cadfael's relationship with God, Church, the Benedictine order, and the world he left behind. Anita M. Vickers's "The Role of Religion in the Cadfael Series" shows us how Cadfael evolved from the crusader into the soldier of Christ, resolutely fighting moral, physical, and political evil wherever he finds it. She investigates Cadfael's conflict between his religious vows of stability and fidelity to his Benedictine brotherhood and his sense of fatherhood to his imprisoned son. In her essay on Cadfael's vocation, Judith J. Kollmann considers the role of the abbot as spiritual father in the *The Rule of Saint Benedict,* especially concentrating on Cadfael's sense of vocation and the question of his "mysticism." In his essay "The Moral World of Brother Cadfael," Anthony Hopkins analyzes the "morally complicated, fundamentally imperfect world" of Cadfael and how he brings about not only a restoration to order but an improvement on order. Carol A. Mylod extends the image of fatherhood in her article on "Fathers in the Cadfael Chronicles" by citing examples of ineffective parenting. She also analyzes how often Cadfael plays "father" as well as "father confessor" to the young Hugh Beringar, to the young lovers in distress, and to the covey of younger Benedictine novices. My article on the persistent presence of lepers, beggars, and pilgrims attempts to explain why the beggar-saints held more interest for Cadfael than the more mundane saints.

The second section of essays deals with how the author incorporates Cadfael's particular talents with his call to ministry of the spiritual and the corporal works of mercy. Although conscious of being a citizen of God's universe, Cadfael is no less conscious of his duties as a citizen of the tumultuous world of twelfth-century England. While the demands of the secular world often intrude on the peace of Cadfael's life, workshop, and vocation, they also provide the basis for the mysteries themselves; thus, the socio-political tension between England and Wales contributes heavily to the stories to affect Cadfael's actions. Kayla McKinney Wiggins's article on the many roles of Cadfael ably explains why Cadfael must juggle his religious vows, his Welsh nationalism, his understanding of Celtic marriage customs, and his fidelity to English law and justice with nimble skill—and why he must do so while retaining his sense of balance. Marcia J. Songer extends Cadfael's socio-political world by detailing how Peters wove historical fact into believable fiction by analyzing the characters of the two royal contenders, Stephen and Maud, and how the squabbles of the cousins changed the fate of England. Margaret Lewis, whose authorized biography of Edith Pargeter has become the definitive sourcebook for the author's life, capsulizes Cadfael's allegience to his Welsh origins by explaining the complicated political arena of the times.

Where the spiritual works of mercy enjoin Cadfael to admonish the sinner, to instruct the ignorant, and to forgive all injuries, it is the corporal works of mercy—to feed the hungry, to clothe the naked, to visit the sick—which enlist his craftsmanship in herbs and nourish his contributions to the mission of mercy held so dear by his Benedictine community. Margaret Baker investigates both Cadfael's role as an herbalist and as a detective by analyzing where Pargeter/Peters accumulated firsthand information on herbs. Carol A. Mylod explores Peters's use of the specific sense of sight as an indication of moral and physical health in her short stories about Cadfael's origins, *A Rare Benedictine.*

Although Peters's creation of Cadfael's world lends itself to scholarly analysis, untangling the author's creative process is rather like Cadfael's creation of a new cordial; the ingredients and proportions of the cordial—mystery, romance, compassion, humor, logic—must be followed to assure its efficacy. The distillation of such a cordial may be lengthy and sometimes painful in the learning but the efficacy of the cordial is never in doubt.

Peters's creation of Cadfael's world is effected by her attention to details so tangible that the reader can almost feel the rough wool about her character's neck and the coarse sandals rubbing blisters on his chilblained feet. With Brother Cadfael, the reader feels the biting cold along the drafty stone monastery corridors, sees the feeble winter light slipping through narrow windows, inhales the lush scents of new-mown hay in abbey meadows, hears the gurgle of the river Severn winding by Shrewsbury, reverberates to the dull clip-clop of the horses' hooves of travelers, tastes the coolly pungent cordial slip down a fevered throat, and smells the potent balms and the decaying bodies in the leperhouse of Saint Giles.

For only when the mystery has been solved, only when Cadfael's ministry has distributed justice tinged with mercy, only when Hugh Beringar and Abbot Radulfus agree, only then will peace be restored to Brother Cadfael's world. For the reader, the restoration of that orderly, peaceful balance is as smooth and soothing as Cadfael's cordials.

Note

1. Sue Feder, the editor of *Most Loving, Mere Folly: The Journal of the Ellis Peters's Appreciation Society,* interviewed Edith Pargeter for the journal.

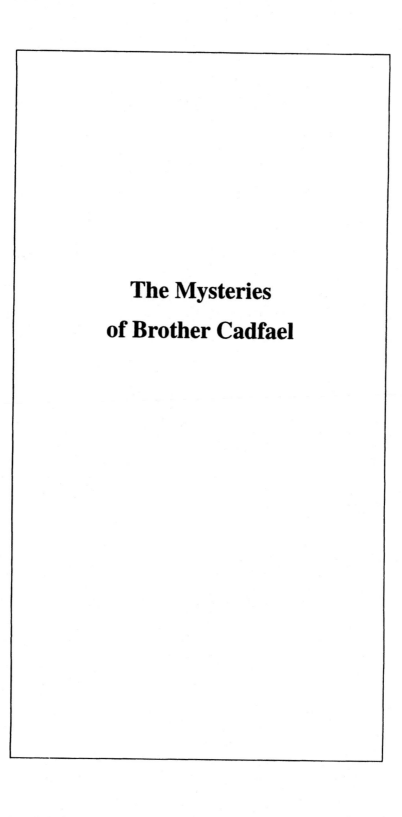

The Mysteries
of Brother Cadfael

The Role of Religion in the Cadfael Series

Anita M. Vickers

At first glance, Ellis Peters's celebrated Brother Cadfael mysteries are a deftly written, engaging series popular with critics and the general reading public alike. On the surface, the writing follows many of the conventions of the detective novel set within a singular historical time period. Assuredly, the choice of a shrewd, discerning monk as sleuth in a series that numbered twenty novels and one book of short stories yields the locus of the series' appeal. Crusader, sea captain, father, cloistered monk, herbalist, apostate, detective: these are but a few of the myriad representations Peters employs in delineating her most famous and successful detective.

But the series is neither exclusively a whodunit (one theme, one intent) nor is it an interweaving of various—but equally important—motifs. Instead, the series is more analogous to a medieval palimpsest where texts are stratified, sometimes completely obliterated, yet sometimes discernible with astounding clarity. Like a palimpsest there are levels of textuality within the chronicles, some obscured, others conclusively evident. Carefully delineated characterizations (especially of Cadfael), accurate historical settings, and intriguing whodunit plots have, unequivocally, taken the forefront in the series as a whole. But beneath these elements remains the traces of the infrastructure of the novels, that is, the religious component.

Religion may, at first, appear to be a propitious device. Indeed, making Cadfael a twelfth-century Benedictine[1] in war-torn England affords Peters what at first appears to be an effective gimmick, one which would set this series apart from other successful contemporary detective novels. Notwithstanding the nature of Cadfael's religious calling, his life within the monastery, and the issues that emanate from the ecclesiastical are never obfuscated by the main text. Certainly the mysteries themselves, the political intrigues, the rich delineation of personages (both fictional and historical alike) predominate the novels. But as the original text of a palimpsest does, at times, becomes manifest, so does the role of religion become illuminated throughout the texts of this series.

Conceivably, it is serendipitous that Peters makes Cadfael a Benedictine.[2] Overall, Benedictine life represented a radical departure from earlier monastic orders; that is, Benedictines are cenobitic (living in a community) as opposed to the earlier eremitic (that is, solitary, which, in Benedict's time, was the most prevalent form of monastic life). Benedict prescribed a life that was neither austere nor penitential. Conversely, the founder's vision was of a community of cenobites "serving as Christ's soldiers under a rule or abbot" (qtd. in Butler 26). Such a community would be circumscribed by an entirely common life: prayer, work, meals, and dormitory (Butler 27).

As soldiers for Christ, Benedictines are expected to adhere strictly to the spiritual principles of the Rule: silence, communal stability, work (albeit in correlation to prayer and reading of Scripture), humility, and obedience. Although the Rule determines the tenets of Benedictine monasticism, it is basically loosely constructed. Interpretation and enforcement are generally left to the abbot's judgment. Thus the monastery becomes both a spiritual army and family, the abbot simultaneously functioning as commander and father.

Such a tenuous structure of the Benedictines (as opposed to the more rigid, exacting monastic models) provides Peters with several advantages when delineating the microcosm of the Abbey of Saints Peter and Paul and its environs. The Benedictine emphasis on useful work (those who were not assigned to theological or scholastic endeavors were expected to engage in less esoteric pursuits, such as cooking, cleaning, and gardening) furnishes Cadfael with a natural vocation within his religious vocation. As the monasterial gardener/herbalist, Cadfael becomes the equivalent of a medieval physician, one whose services are in demand by the religious and the secular communities alike. Not only does Cadfael's expertise proffer a forensic skill that greatly aids in the solution of crimes, but it allows Peters to move her detective freely outside the abbey's community. (Even though Benedictines were considered to be the most liberal in their authority, as cenobites they were customarily expected to remain within the confines of the monastery.)

Ordinarily, the religious element within the series serves as some sort of chronological point of reference. (For example, the chapters in *The Sanctuary Sparrow* have titles such as "Saturday, from Prime to Noon," a definite allusion to recitation of the Office.) Sometimes the religious environment may even offer a commentary on the foibles of humanity. (The monks of the Abbey of Saints Peter and Paul are, at many times, guilty of being quarrelsome, petty, and imperious—far from being the stereotypical saintly lot.) Moreover, religion is in palimpsest in many of the novels, abrading the primary text, the mystery plot. Sometimes religion does, in fact, become the focal point of the plot, notably in the first novel and last two novels of the series, *A Morbid Taste for Bones* (1977), *The Holy Thief* (1992), and *Brother Cadfael's Penance* (1994).

The first novel in the series, *A Morbid Taste for Bones,* originally was not intended as a launch for a new series. Perhaps this is why the crime itself centers on a religious issue, that of the veneration of saints and their relics within the Catholic Church, rather than some of the more secular-related crimes in subsequent books. The motive for murder and Cadfael's involvement in the coverup of the identity of the murderer—and the nature of the murderer's own untimely demise—stem from the corruption and unbridled ambition in relation to the need to acquire relics.

Briefly, the Abbey has found itself to be bereft of a first-class relic.[3] The ever-scheming and consistently ambitious Prior Robert has decided that the Abbey's lack of a first-class relic is ignominious and must be immediately rectified. (In Prior Robert's somewhat dubious defense, the Abbey would be in violation of the 787 Second Council of Nicaea's pronouncement that before any church could be consecrated, relics had to be installed. The lack of any relics would be in direct violation of this decree, although a whole body would not have been required—a bone would have sufficed.) With the help of the sycophantic Brother Jerome, Prior Robert concocts a plan to rectify the situation post haste. Through careful investigation, the Prior had discovered that a first-class relic, the body of Saint Winifred, is lying in a grave in the Welsh parish of Gwytherin. The grave itself is sadly in need of restoration. Assuming that the neglect of the grave reflects the Welsh attitude toward their saint (ergo, the Welsh have neglected to venerate her), a contingent from the monastery, headed by the Prior and including Cadfael (who, as a native Welshman, would serve as interpreter) sets out for Gwytherin to bring back this most holy relic. Unfortunately, urgency and immediacy supersede true devotion or spiritual awareness. In the words of the more worldly Brother John (Cadfael's gardening assistant):

He [Prior Robert] had it all planned beforehand. . . . That was all a show, all that wonder and amazement, and asking who Saint Winifred was, and where to find her. He knew it all along. He'd already picked her out from those he's discovered neglected in Wales, and *decided she was the one most likely to be available, as well as the one to shed most lustre on him.* (*Bones* 17; emphasis added)

But the Welsh are not so eager to give up the body of their beloved little saint, especially to an *English* monastery. Led by their powerful landowner, Lord Rhisiart, the people of Gwytherin resist the efforts of the monks to take Saint Winifred's remains to Shrewsbury, and thus out of Wales forever. Prior Robert's offer to pay for the remains is seen as the final insult. The negotiations are deadlocked.

Auspiciously, Rhisiart is found the next day with an arrow imbedded in his breast. Prior Robert sees this as retribution from the saint for someone who interfered with the monks' holy duties. Cadfael thinks otherwise. A falsely accused suspect is arrested for the crime. With the help of the suspect and his love interest (the daughter of the murder victim), Cadfael exacts a confession from the real malefactor, an overly ambitious young monk prone to highly theatrical antics, Brother Columbanus.

Through Cadfael's canny discernment, both as detective and student of human nature, the reader learns that Columbanus murdered Rhisiart not out of some misguided notion of holy duty, but because he knew that his part in acquiring a first-class relic might lead to a rapid promotion within the ranks of the monastery: sub-prior, then prior, finally to abbot.

At first it may seem that the murder involves more worldly issues than theological. Brother Columbanus is a flawed monk, a product of the discriminatory social strata of twelfth-century England. (He is of Norman blood, thus a member of the reigning aristocracy of the time.) What motivates him is blind ambition and ruthless zeal. Neither he nor Prior Robert (also a Norman) are concerned with the fundamental reasons as to why Saint Winifred should be venerated, only the how (and what that would mean for the glory of the Abbey—and themselves). In addition, this is a common motif in many detective novels: the allure of an object, one that is purported to have some sort of mystical power, to lead someone to commit murder.

Aside from addressing worldly issues and following generic conventions, the veneration of the saints is truly the crux of this novel, particularly in light of the fact that, by this time, the veneration of saints and their relics had reached epidemic proportions. Enshrined relics were viewed by most of the populace as having miraculous powers. (Not surprisingly, in the novel's closing chapter, two years after the murder and the supposed transfer of the relic to Shrewsbury, Cadfael learns that many marvelous cures have occurred at the Gwytherin gravesite. The blind can now see, the crippled can now walk. Women dying in childbirth, after lying across the grave, have delivered whole, healthy children and survived themselves. This, of course, is in direct contrast to the paltry "cures" that have transpired at the spurious reliquary at Shrewsbury.)

Notwithstanding the more temporal advantages of having relics enshrined (pilgrimages to shrines usually meant a fortuitous escalation in prestige—and income—for the site of relics and reliquaries), there were spiritual advantages. The faithful regarded the miraculous events attributed to these shrines as unquestionable evidence of the presence of Christ in the material world through the intervention of His saints.

The teachings of the Church are quite clear here. Those who are declared to be saints by the Church are those, who by heroic virtue, are in heaven and are in union with the living ("the communion of saints"). Based on scripture, the Church proclaims that the saints watch over the living, that they solicitously pray for the living, and, consequently, that the living can pray with them (Lukefahr 168). Accordingly, they serve as powerful intercessors on the behalf of the living.

Relics, whether they be first, second, or third class, are merely records that, not only did the saint once exist, but that he or she is with God. Irrefutably, it is the saints themselves who are the focus of reverence; the relics are only signs of the saints' powers.

And this is the true impetus for the action in the novel. The monks of Shrewsbury—excluding Cadfael—have misinterpreted the Church's teachings. Prior Robert and his cohorts revere the relic, not the saint herself. Cadfael sagaciously observes that he could "never see why a man can't reverence his favourite saint without wanting to fondle her bones, but there's great rivalry for such relics among the abbeys these days" (*Bones* 61). Hence, the tacit explanation for this most peculiar book title.

It is the relatively less-than-scholarly Cadfael whose theology on this subject is sound, not the learned Prior Robert. Although Peters takes great pains to portray Cadfael as an atypical monk (he prefers to sleep during chapter, not much account is given to his participation in the Mass or the recitation of the Office), by having Cadfael make such a profound statement she evinces his sincere devotion to his faith and his vocation. As a Benedictine, the soldier of the world turned soldier of Christ, he knows he must obey a higher commander than the abbey administrators, and that commander is Saint Winifred herself, who, as a saint, is metaphorically a high ranking officer in Christ's army.

Saint Winifred speaks through her impersonator during a plot designed to extract a confession from Brother Columbanus. Swathed in white grave clothes and carefully veiled, Sioned Rhisiart, posing as Winifred, confronts her father's murderer with a dreadful accusation:

I never wished to leave my resting-place here in Gwytherin. Who told you otherwise but your own devil of ambition? I laid my hand upon a good man, and sent him out to be my champion, and on this day he has been buried here, a martyr for my sake. The sin is recorded in heaven, there is no hiding-place for you. Why . . . have you killed my servant Rhisiart? (*Bones* 165)

At first Cadfael deduces that Sioned had ad-libbed this speech; she had merely been caught up in the passion of the moment. But after questioning her afterwards, it becomes clear to the brotherly sleuth that these were not words of Sioned's cognizance. He interprets this as Saint Winifred speaking through Sioned, thus using the grieving daughter as the instrument to render justice. If Saint Winifred does not want her bones moved from Wales, then Cadfael, ever the obedient soldier, will comply with her wishes.

Bolstered by the authority which he views Saint Winifred has conferred upon him, the wily monk sees this as a solution to a more recent, pressing problem. When Columbanus realizes that the apparition is really flesh-and-bone, he tries to stab Sioned with the same dagger with which he killed her father. Sioned's lover, the falsely accused Engelard, grabs Columbanus and shakes him furiously, breaking the malefactor's neck. Now there is a body to dispose of and an accidental killing to coverup. What better scheme but to lift the seal of the reliquary, replace the remains of Saint Winifred with those of Columbanus, and restore the saint to her Welsh resting place?

A clever stratagem, but there is still one predicament to deal with: How to explain Columbanus' disappearance? Once more, Peters turns to religious illusion to solve the problem. She has Cadfael engineer a most elaborate ruse—it will appear to all that Columbanus has been assumed into heaven.[4] His habit, even his undergarments, are carefully positioned as if a man were wearing them, kneeling in a posture of extreme reverence. Prior Robert, exercising his authority, declares to the assembly that

He [Columbanus] has been marvellously favoured, and his most demanding prayers heard. Let us say a Mass here for Brother Columbanus. Before we take up the blessed lady who has made him her herald, and go to make known this *miracle of faith*. (*Bones* 185; emphasis added)

For the most part, the monastic community—and the Shrewsbury denizens—believe that the first-class relics of Saint Winifred are safely installed beneath the altar. The "assumption" of Brother Columbanus has entered the local lore, attributed to just another of the miracles ascribed to the saint. Only Cadfael, his friend and confidante, Hugh Beringar, sheriff of Shrewsbury, and the people of Gwytherin know the true story. Obviously, "heavenly justice" (as redressed by Cadfael) in this novel transcends ecclesiastical and secular justice.

Throughout the series, Cadfael exhibits a genuine devotion toward the little Welsh saint. Even though he knows the truth, he feels her presence within the monastery walls and often prays for her intercession in many of the problems that crop up within the series. (And, consistently aware of Saint Winifred's nationalistic propensity—after all, she preferred an ignominious grave in Wales over an elaborate enshrinement in England—Cadfael always prays to her, not in English, but in the north Welsh of Gwynedd.) Because of his role as her agent in the first novel, he feels that he and Saint Winifred have a special bond and that the saint has bestowed favors on the abbey as a result. Not until the penultimate novel, however, does the saint take an active role in the mystery.

In *The Holy Thief,* Saint Winifred becomes what appears to be an informant to the crime, albeit a most holy one. Within a plot characterized by multiple crimes (theft of a first-class relic, an efficient, and therefore, successful crime ring composed of footpads, a murder, and attempted murder[s]), Cadfael (as well as other members of the monastic community) resorts to what may be seen as a desperate measure: *sortes Biblicae.*

Sortes Biblicae, as depicted in this novel, is a method of invoking heavenly guidance, or, as Hugh Beringar rather crassly defines it: "the common practice of reading the future be opening the Evangel [the Christian gospels] blindly, and laying a finger on the page" (*Thief* 119). In twelfth-century England this was practiced for an assortment of problems, predicaments, or ecclesiastical issues. For instance, Cadfael, in elucidating Beringar on the finer points of the practice, cites several historical precedents for *sortes Biblicae* during the consecration of a bishop although he admits that he has never been present for any of these; consequently, what he relates can be aptly termed as hearsay. Notwithstanding, the examples he cites are engaging, bordering on historical rumormongering: The disgraced Bishop Roger of Salisbury's *sortes* prophesied, "'Bind his hands and feet, and cast him into outer darkness,'" and the equally discredited Henry of Winchester received a verse from the Gospel of Matthew enjoining the faithful that in the future false prophets would become multitudinous (*Thief* 120).

With the argument for the veracity of *sortes Biblicae* now convincingly marshalled with historic precedents, Peters is able to incorporate this method within the storyline. When Cadfael subsequently uses *sortes Biblicae* to invoke Saint Winifred's guidance in solving the mystery of the murder of Aldhelm, a seemingly harmless and gentle young man, the response he receives should be taken literally as fact by the reader. His finger lands upon a cryptic passage from Matthew 10:21, translated by Cadfael from Latin into English as "and the brother shall deliver up the brother to death" (*Thief* 144). Thus it appears that he is provided with a exceptionally vital clue that will prove instrumental in the solution of the mystery.

Moreover, Cadfael is not the only petitioner who is offered this clue. After the assembled community meets in prayer, the pages of the Gospel turn as if by magic, remaining open on the Gospel of Matthew, a blackthorn bud resting on Chapter 10, verse 21. Father Abbot Radulfus, long established within the series as a exemplary leader and Benedic-tine,[5] forthrightly declares that "'I take the omen as grace. And I accept this bud as the finger of truth thus manifested'" (*Thief* 157).

But Saint Winifred's "clue" is actually a red herring. Cadfael understandably interprets the message as a case of mistaken identity. Aldhelm's cloak and hood, seen in a nighttime rainfall, could easily be taken for a Benedictine cowl and habit. He deduces that the real target was Brother Tutilo, a mischief maker from a rival abbey—and in one respect his deduction is correct. Saint Winifred's message does, consequently, elicit a confession from Brother Jerome, who admits that he waited in the dark for Brother Tutilo with the intent to confront him.

Having what he thought was Tutilo in his sight, Jerome had angrily picked up a branch and struck his quarry. Upon closer scrutiny, he realized that the now-fallen man was not Tutilo. In fear and repentance (believing Aldhelm to be dead), Brother Jerome ran back to the abbey in shame, hiding his guilty secret until this climactic moment. But he is not the murderer.

The real murderer, Benezet, servant to a visiting troubadour by day, footpad by night, finds the unconscious Aldhelm and seizes this opportunity to dispatch a potential witness to his nefarious activities. So, in a sense, what appeared to be a solution to the main mystery, in fact, has led to the solution. Saint Winifred's message has caused a sinful monk to repent and confess his role in Aldhelm's demise—and that confession subsequently clears a falsely accused suspect (Tutilo), leading to the discovery of the real murderer.

This is a most heterodox turn of events and a deviation from formula. Once again the issue of religion (in this case, the purification of a diseased soul) arises from the text, abrading the mystery at hand. What is of prime importance here is not bringing a lost soul (criminal) to justice, but the salvation of a straying monk, one who by default is under the protection of Saint Winifred. As in all good mysteries, however, every conflict is reconciled, the murderer apprehended and brought to justice (Benezet), a young man whose true calling is not monastic forsakes the cowl in favor of a secular vocation (Tutilo), and a pathetic monk has been humbled, forgiven, and perchance will live closer in spirit to Benedict's Rule.

Overall, *The Holy Thief* sustains the optimistic tone throughout the series. The Cadfael mysteries are, at times, characterized by an almost lighthearted quality. Brother Cadfael's wit, rascality, and, of course, the allusions to his romantic escapades as a younger man provide a cathartic release to all the murder and mayhem in Shrewsbury. For the most part, religion is the basis of characterization, atmosphere, and action. Crises are met with stoic faith and aided by heavenly intervention. Cadfael's vocation is a source of security and serenity in his later years. There is never any indication that he has regrets or that he would ever return to secular life. That is, until the twentieth Chronicle, *Brother Cadfael's Penance*.

The religious infrastructure is truly illuminated in this novel. The last chronicle is the most disturbing in tone, intent, and design. As the title indicates, the focus is not on a mystery but on Cadfael's spiritual fitness. The mystery may be afoot, but religion supersedes any sleuthing that takes place. Indeed, it appears that there is very little detective work in regards to the murder. (This time the victim is a treacherous castellan, Brien de Soulis.) In fact, Cadfael does not solve the mystery. Rather, the murderer, a grieving mother who had efficiently dispatched de Soulis out of revenge for her illegitimate son's death, confesses her guilt to the monk with no prompting on his part. Even though the reader is provided a few clues along the way to the identity of the murderer, the mystery itself becomes of tertiary importance, supplanted by two more compelling issues: Cadfael's rescue of his son and the restoration of his soul.

These two issues are interminably intertwined throughout the novel. Arguably, the emotional aspects of paternal devotion and loyalty heighten the rich structure and characterization of the mystery, but it is Cadfael's internal conflict that is the actual theme of the work. This is not the Cadfael of the other nineteen chronicles. Instead, this is a man whose spirituality is being sorely tested—and to what end? Here lies the *true* mystery.

Now in November of 1145, England is still engaged in the civil strife between the Empress Maud and King Stephen. Due to the perfidy of one of Maud's most trusted supporters, Philip FitzRobert, thirty knights in the empress's service have been imprisoned, among them Cadfael's illegitimate son (sired during his crusading days), Olivier de Bretagne. Cadfael's dilemma thus lies in his decision whether to remain within the walls of the monastery, leaving Olivier's fate to chance, or to actively work for his release—and forsaking the monastic life, perhaps temporarily, perhaps for good. He petitions Radulfus to allow him to embark on a quest to find his son and to the council at Coventry so that he may entreat Maud and Stephen to intervene for Olivier's freedom.[6]

Radulfus, after some deliberation, judiciously grants permission with a few caveats. First, he reminds Cadfael that his monastic vows are binding, that he willingly chose to surrender the secular for the religious and that choice cannot be easily rescinded. Second, Cadfael must return when the council disperses. If he decides to pursue his quest then " 'you go as your

own man, none of mine. Without my leave or my blessing'"
(*Penance* 17). With that profound admonition weighing on his
soul, Cadfael sets off to find his son.

But his efforts at Coventry come to nought. Now he is
faced with an even greater dilemma: Should he disregard Radulfus's edict and continue his search? Does his duty as a Welsh
father supplant his duty as a Benedictine brother? If he does
resolve to proceed, he will be in a state of apostasy with spiritual
repercussions most dire. As he habitually does throughout the
series, Cadfael searches for peace and guidance in his usual
manner. He decides to pray.

Unfortunately, the solace Cadfael has sought and procured
in the earlier novels is not available to him. Away from Saint
Winifred's shrine he enters a priory church, but becomes acutely
aware that the tranquility and comfort is not the same:

There were now quiet corners enough within there for every soul who
desired a holy solitude and the peopled silence of the presence of God.
In entering any other church but his own he missed, for one moment,
the small stone altar and the chased reliquary where Saint Winifred
was not, and yet was. Just to set eyes on it was to kindle a little living
fire within his heart. Here he must forgo that particular consolation,
and submit to an unfamiliar benediction. Nevertheless, there was an
answer here for every need. (*Penance* 61)

The answer is, however, not an easy one, leaving Cadfael to
continue to wrestle with his conscience almost up to the last page.
But as in all well-wrought mysteries, the author provides subtle
clues to the reader what the final outcome will be. Although
Peters deftly limns Cadfael's deviation from his vows as a crisis
of spiritual ethics, she also renders a consistent and entirely plau-
sible delineation of some stability of character.

Though he is technically an apostate, he still keeps the
Office, not out of habit but out of sincere devotion. Even his
constant war of conscience throughout the novel is testament to
his religious fortitude and integrity. A man so torn and uneasy
about his decision to relinquish his monastic responsibilities is
one who would not abandon the cowl. In fact, in his departing
words to Radulfus, Cadfael reminds his superior that "'it is writ-

ten in the Rule [and Cadfael reveres the Rule above everything] that the brother who by his own wrong choice has left the monastery may be received again, even to the third time, at a price'" *(Penance* 17).

Once Olivier is freed, the murder of de Soulis solved, the once perfidious Philip FitzRobert safe from execution because of his treason (in fact, he, too, has taken religious vows), and all other intrigues satisfactorily resolved, the apostate returns to his spiritual haven. Although he is neither repentant nor supplicant, Cadfael is welcomed by Radulfus back into the community. His closing thoughts aptly summarize the depth and intensity of his decision to return:

Cadfael drew breath and remembered. A way to go, when he despaired of princes. Though he would still find the princes of this world handling and mishandling the cause of Christendom as they mishandled the cause of England. All the more to be desired was this order and tranquility within the pale, where the battle of heaven and hell was fought without bloodshed, with the weapons of the mind and the soul. *(Penance* 255)

The soldier of Christ has returned to serve his commander in the true spirit of the Rule. The palimpsest is now completely recovered: a fitting end to a superior medieval mystery series.

Notes

1. Benedictines are not a singular order. Rather, they are a confederation of religious men and women who follow the Rule of Benedict of Nursia (480-547). The confederation comprises autonomous monastic communities that are affixed to other monasteries by a indeterminate jurisdiction and a collective dedication to the Rule.

2. Peters set the series within the confines of her native Shropshire with remarkable historical accuracy, including the presence of a Benedictine abbey during the Middle Ages. In fact, the Benedictines had a long, established history in England. As early as 596, the Benedictines had been charged by Pope Gregory the Great to evangelize

Britain. At first their efforts were successful, particularly in southern England with the Jutes. The headstrong denizens, however, eventually lapsed back into paganism, especially the Cornish and the Welsh contingents. According to Cuthbert Butler, who cites the most renowned of the English Benedictines, The Venerable Bede, as his source, the Benedictines were the first Christian missionaries in England, but the eventual conversion of the island was due more to the efforts of the Hiberno-Scottish monks and by independent missionaries from the continent (315). Nevertheless, by the twelfth century, Christianity had flourished in England, with the Benedictines firmly ensconced in southern England.

3. The Catholic Church recognizes three classes of relics: first-class, either the remains of saint or a part, such as a bone chip; second-class, an article intrinsically identified with a saint or with Christ; and third-class, an article authenticated as having touched a saint, such as a rosary or prayerbook. In this novel, the contention between the monks of Shrewsbury and the Welsh over the remains of Saint Winifred is a highly charged one, since this would be a first-class relic.

4. Assumption of a body into heaven plays a significant role in Catholic teaching, the most notable example being the dogma of the Assumption of the Blessed Virgin Mary. Although generally accepted as doctrine during Cadfael's time, this was not declared an official Church teaching until 1950 by Pope Pius XII. But there are Biblical references to assumption of bodies (thereby escaping the death experience) as well. In Genesis 5:24, Enoch, the father of Methuselah, described as a righteous man, who at the age of sixty-five walks with God and is taken to heaven. In 2 Kings 2:11, the prophet Elijah also does not experience death. Instead, he is taken up to heaven in a whirlwind. Hence, Cadfael's design has scriptural and doctrinal precedents and would be believed by the monks and the Welsh community alike.

5. Another issue tacitly alluded to within the series is the role of the abbot in the Benedictine community. The Abbey has three heads (one acting) during Cadfael's career as amateur detective. The first, Heribert, serves as abbot in the first two novels and is removed in the third. A kindly, old man, he lacks the administrative abilities and the political acumen to be a good commanding officer in this army of Christ. His substitute in *Monk's-Hood*, Prior Robert, although eager to assume leadership—perhaps too eager—lacks the qualities a good abbot must have as well. Radulfus, however, is the quintessential

Benedictine—pious, just, intelligent, and discerning. His character also functions as a model. He is the Benedictine Cadfael could be with more restraint. But Cadfael throughout the series struggles with adherence to the Rule—and particularly the vow of obedience. A man of the world now cloistered off from that world, he sometimes chafes under authority (particularly during Prior Robert's brief tenure as head), sometimes thwarting what he views as unreasonable edicts quite successfully.

6. Olivier's reaction to Cadfael's sacrifice bears mentioning here. Initially, he is outraged. For Olivier, Cadfael's apostasy is an unfair burden. He feels that, because he is the impetus of Cadfael's self-sacrificial decision, he has denied his father the peace and tranquility he deserves in his twilight years.

Works Cited

The Bible.

Butler, Cuthbert. *Benedictine Monachism: Studies in Benedictine Life and Rule.* 1919. New York: Barnes & Noble, 1961.

Lukefahr, Oscar. *"We Believe . . ." A Survey of the Catholic Faith.* Liguori, MO: Liguori, 1990.

Peters, Ellis. *Brother Cadfael's Penance.* New York: Mysterious, 1994.

——. *The Holy Thief.* 1992. New York: Mysterious, 1994.

——. *Monk's-Hood.* 1980. New York: Mysterious, 1992.

——. *A Morbid Taste for Bones.* 1977. New York: Mysterious, 1994.

Brother Cadfael's Vocation:
Benedictine Monasticism
in the Cadfael Chronicles

Judith J. Kollmann

In *Mysterium and Mystery: The Clerical Crime Novel* (1989), William Spencer argues that Ellis Peters's "series has never satisfactorily come to grips with its theology. Essentially, the weakness of this well written and in many ways superlative series is that, even though it deals with a medieval monk, it has no notion at all of mystical worship. . . . In the Cadfael series mystical worship is depicted as either a sham or a transport into pseudosexual rapture. . . . Mystical devotion, as an authentic response, is a completely absent element" (69). Spencer has missed Peters's intent: the Brother Cadfael series is firmly based on the sophisticated Benedictine tradition, which was not developed for the purpose of mystical worship, but rather to sustain a community whose main *raison d'être* is the spiritual development of each individual as individual. Such development does not preclude mystical experience; instead, it recognizes that mystical experience is one of a number of modes for spiritual development. In any event, authentic mystical experience is very much an element in Cadfael's life. Peters was well aware of Benedictine tradition, incorporating and adapting it with meticulous care, and an exploration of the Benedictine environment of these novels is in order here. First there will be a brief summary of the nature and the development of monasticism in the West; second, there will be a brief look at twelfth-century English Benedictine monasticism in general, and Shrewsbury Abbey in particular. Third, there will be an exploration of the specific monastic issues with which the Cadfael chronicles deal: namely,

27

the question of vocation and the nature of Cadfael's spiritual experience.

By the fourth century C.E., Saint Augustine of Hippo (b. 354) had developed a concept of monastic life that was characterized by intellectual activity and meditation. He also understood that the three monastic vows—of celibacy, poverty and obedience—constituted the essential disciplines for the monk. Benedict (ca. 470-547) inherited and valued the disciplines of mind and spirit as well as the three vows, incorporating all of this into the Rule of Benedict, but he added to them communal organization and manual labor. Each of these not only provided a vital necessity (a governance structure and a self-sufficient monastery); both also became integral to spiritual development *vis-à-vis* Bernard's concept of the office of abbot. The intent of the Rule was to make every aspect of the monk's life integral to a life of prayer. Benedict divided the monk's day into three activities: first, the worship of the community in communal prayer (also called the Opus Dei, Work of God, or the Divine Office); second, solitary, meditative reading or prayer; and third, labor. Thus, manual labor became a form of religious exercise. The intent was that "the life within the monastery is a common life of absolute regularity, of strict discipline, of unvarying routine. The whole ordering of the day is concerned with furthering the spiritual welfare of those who form the family" (Knowles 4).

Of the three divisions, liturgical (or public) prayer was the most important. Benedict wrote "Ergo nihil Operi Dei praeponatur" ("Therefore nothing shall take precedence of the Work of God," *Regula* xliii, 5). However, as Dom David Knowles points out, "The Opus Dei is . . . only a part, though in itself the most noble part, of the monk's daily employment; it is not the *raison d'être* of the institute" (5). The daily reading, for which approximately four hours were allocated, meant that every monk who could learn to read was literate. The monk's labor might be field labor; however, "labor" could also mean any craft necessary to sustain monastic life, such as music; book production (binding, illumination or writing); wheel wrighting; cooking; sewing; smithing; care of the sick; or, of course, growing and preparing medicinal herbs. Benedict's vision was that, while serving his community, the monk also served his own spiritual needs: each of his daily activities balanced and flowed into one another.

The Rule also promoted an ascetic way of life. The monk was to eat two meals a day (only one during the penitential seasons of Advent and Lent); he was to own nothing; he was to rise at midnight to begin the day with the first liturgical prayer. However, the Rule was also full of common sense: each meal was to offer two dishes so that everyone would have a choice. Each monk was to be adequately shod and clothed, and, should he have to travel, he was to be provided with better quality of clothing than he normally wore in the monastery. Extremes of any kind were not encouraged.

The Rule of Benedict consists of seventy-three rules which became the foundation of the Benedictine Order, and is an intensely practical outline designed to allow any man who, having been called to the life of a monk, could achieve spiritual maturity regardless of intellect, abilities, or social class. It was understood that a monk's life was a process of development, and the person responsible for the spiritual growth of every brother was the abbot. Benedict pointed out that the word "abbot" was derived from the Hebrew *abba,* which means "father," and, of course, that was precisely what an abbot was. However, in addition the abbot was responsible for the administration of the entire establishment. Thus, the ideal abbot was one who was a superbly spiritual man and simultaneously a gifted administrator.

To this man each monk made his vow of obedience because, as Louis Bouyer expresses it, "Only obedience will form the monk to the basic virtues, which now appears as humility. . . . Benedict's whole doctrine of spiritual progress consists in his teaching on the degree of humility. Humility, which is openness to grace, perfect disposability to the divine will, manifested in all things, becomes the mother of perfection itself, that is the flowering of true charity" (517).

The Brother Cadfael series takes place during the reign of two abbots: Heribert (1127-1138) and Radulfus (1138-c1148). Both abbots are historical figures; fictionally speaking, Heribert's tenancy extends through *A Morbid Taste for Bones* and *One Corpse Too Many*; he is deposed (by a papal legate) in the third novel, *Monk's-Hood.* Radulfus is abbot for the rest of the series.

However, there is a third in the would-be-abbot, Prior Robert Pennant. Historically Robert Pennant succeeded Radulfus, ruling from c.1148-1167. Not much is known about these historical personages, except that Ordericus Vitalis described Heribert as one who "usurped the rudder of the infant establishment" (Whiteman 171). Ordericus's choice of verb clearly implies the real Heribert was conniving and ambitious. However, the fictional Heribert is a kindly, spiritual man who "was old, of mild nature and pliant, a gentle grey ascetic very wishful of peace and harmony around him. His figure was unimpressive, though his face was beguiling in its anxious sweetness" (*Bones* 6). He is somewhat dominated by Prior Robert. The historical (and the fictive) Heribert was removed from office because he did not acknowledge King Stephen's right to the throne quickly enough following the siege of Shrewsbury, and upon his deposition became a simple choir monk who died in that position three years later. Peters's Heribert was happy to be relieved of his responsibilities so he could practice the spirituality for which he had longed.

Prior Robert is one of Peters's secondary continuing characters. He has several useful functions; among these is the fact that he is Heribert's antithesis. Robert is so ambitious that he almost becomes the true villain of the series. He is aided by his loyal shadow, the obsequious and inquisitive Brother Jerome. Robert, with his pride, his legalistic theological rigidity and busy-bodiness, is the manifestation of what can happen to a person whose real vocation is not the cloister but who remains within because he does not have enough personal honesty or introspectiveness to acknowledge his own hypocrisy.

These two extremes, of Heribert, the spiritual but administratively inadequate abbot, on the one hand, and of Prior Robert, the spiritually bankrupt but administratively competent would-be abbot, on the other, flank Radulfus. Each contrasts with him and illuminates him as the ideal abbot, gifted both spiritually and administratively. He runs the abbey efficiently, always aware of everything that happens in his domain and always protecting it. As a prince of the church, he is politically astute in matters involving the country; in *The Heretic's Apprentice*, Canon Gerbert of Canterbury attempts to take control of a young man whom he insists is to be charged with heresy. Radulfus resists this, and instead refers the case to the jurisdiction of his own bishop of Coventry: "A judgment of Solomon, thought Cadfael, well content with his abbot" (53). In affairs between the abbey and local groups, such as the citizens of Shrewsbury, Radulfus protects the abbey's interests and rights but does not ignore the needs of the surrounding community. Thus, when a deputation of citizens in *Saint Peter's Fair* requests a share in the Abbey's profits from the Abbey's Fair, Radulfus listens to the request but refuses to budge on a matter involving the abbey's legal rights. However, he can dispose of the money acquired by the Fair as he pleases, and he chooses to share the profits with the town.

As the spiritual father of Shrewsbury, Radulfus never interferes with the monks unless he is asked. The abbey has a complement of priest-monks who deal with day-to-day spiritual guidance and Radulfus trusts them. However, if a monk asks to see the abbot, Radulfus is always available. Brother Haluin (in *The Confession of Brother Haluin*) believes himself to be dying; he asks that Radulfus and Cadfael hear his confession—Cadfael because Haluin's sin concerns misappropriation of Cadfael's drugs. It is the middle of the night, and Radulfus comes immediately.

Cadfael himself respects Radulfus highly. Perhaps the most significant development in their relationship occurs in *Brother Cadfael's Penance*. Cadfael has discovered that his son, Olivier de Bretagne, has been imprisoned and is being held hostage by persons unknown. Cadfael requests permission to leave the community in order to find Olivier. He makes clear to Radulfus that he will go, whether or not he has permission. Radulfus grants him leave to attend a meeting between King Stephen and the Empress Maud, where Cadfael hopes to learn news of Olivier, but orders him to return at the end of the council. Cadfael indicates that he will not do so if he has not been successful at the meeting. Radulfus responds that Cadfael will then "'go as your own man, none of mine. Without my leave or my blessing'" (17). Cadfael asks: "'Without your prayers?' Radulfus responds: 'Have I said so?'" Cadfael then reminds Radulfus: "'it is written in the Rule that the brother who by his own wrong choice has left the monastery may be received again, even to the third time, at a price. Even penance ends when you shall say: 'It is enough!'" (17).

Cadfael attends the meeting, does not find Olivier, but uncovers hints of his whereabouts. In addition, a murder is committed and one of his old friends, Yves Hugonin, friend and brother-in-law to Olivier, is accused of the murder. In order to free him and find Olivier, Cadfael continues on alone, bereft of his monastery. While Peters emphasizes Cadfael's satisfaction and contentment with his vocation in every novel, in none is his commitment to his order so emphatic, and in none is Cadfael's humility so clearly delineated, although in fact both the depth of his vocation and his spiritual development have been significant factors since the first novel, *A Morbid Taste for Bones*. In *Penance*, Cadfael keeps the Opus Dei, rising at midnight, even though he not only knows himself to be a renegade monk but has admitted as much to his host, Count Philip Fitz Robert. It is the fact that he remains true to his discipline that impresses Philip and eventually allows Cadfael to free his son and to save Philip's life. When at last Cadfael turns for home, he begins a long penitential journey through the winter, arriving at Shrewsbury after the midnight service. He does not presume to go to his own bed; nor does he ask to be received as a guest in the guest house. Instead, he goes in the church, where he lies down outside the choir, taking a cruciform position on the stones.

In the morning Radulfus arrives before anyone else, and finds Cadfael, who says "'Father!' asking nothing, promising nothing, repenting nothing" (254). Radulfus gives him news of the recent events in national politics, in which everything is still unresolved turmoil. Cadfael thinks, "All the more to be desired was this order and tranquillity within the pale, where the battle of heaven and hell was fought without bloodshed, with the weapons of the mind and the soul" (255). Finally, Radulfus utters the words Cadfael had hoped to hear, but which he did not presume to expect: "'It is enough!'"—the formal words that the abbot utters to end a monk's penance. And, as the novel concludes, Radulfus invites Cadfael to "'Get up now, and come with your brothers into the choir'" (255).

Cadfael has here attained true and complete humility: he has made a choice between two duties—staying, as a monk should, within the cloister, or answering the need to be a parent. In either case, he would necessarily make both a right, and a wrong decision. Having made his choice, he cannot repent the right choice, only the wrong. And he can only be what true Benedictine humility is: in a state of being that is nothing except what God wants the person to be. As such, Cadfael has been an instrument of God in solving more than the mystery of where a young man disappeared and liberating him. Cadfael has also saved the life of another young man (Philip, who had imprisoned Olivier). Moreover, Cadfael has been instrumental in the reconciliation between Count Philip and his father, Robert, Duke of Gloucester. Cadfael has served as the medium through which the love of God can work in the world, even though doing so involved the primary sin of the monk—disobedience to his abbot. It is to Radulfus's credit that he places first the fact that he is the shepherd of his monks, and welcomes Cadfael back to his true place, in the choir, the place that belongs to the brethren alone.

By the twelfth century, a steady withdrawal of the abbot, his staff and his servants was taking place. It was a physical withdrawal into a separate residence which could also become a spiritual withdrawal from the bretheren. Radulfus is typical in that he resides in a separate establishment within the monastic walls. In addition, his manner is reserved, but he is not drawn away from his brethren. Rather, he is sensitive: unlike Prior Robert, he understands and respects the need for privacy of personhood. It is also clear he has the trust and respect of his monks, and they are comfortable in coming to him for their deepest spiritual needs. He is a superb portrait of a twelfth-century abbot who balances his position as a prince of the church with an awareness of the needs of each of his monks.

Of course there is far more to a monastery than its abbot and its monks, and during the course of the twenty Cadfael novels Peters explores nearly every aspect of this monastic community that had been built next to the sizable city of Shrewsbury. In fact, nearly all the novels deal in some way with the inevitable interface between a reclusive community and a secular, busy world that breathes all about it.

Of course, the Rule of Benedict stipulates that the monastic community is forbidden to close its gates against the needs of the outside world, and the real "craft" of the monk is constituted of good works. Rule 17 states that it is the monks' responsibility to bury the dead (*One Corpse Too Many*); Rule 16 stipulates the need to visit the sick (*Leper of Saint Giles; Sanctuary Sparrow* and others); Rule 18, the monk is to come to aid those in trouble (*Virgin in the Ice*); not part of the Rule but an aspect of medieval life is the institution of sanctuary, allowing anyone forty days to gather spiritual strength, even if pursued by the law (*Sanctuary Sparrow*). Monastic properties or responsibilities extend into the world: *Monk's-Hood* deals with the practice of exchanging monastically-owned homes for land as a form of easy retirement; *Saint Peter's Fair* with the right of monastic institutions to operate secular income-producing events; *Raven in the Foregate* is concerned with churches owned outside the abbey pale and responsibilities accruing therefrom; *The Rose Rent* and *The Potter's Field* with properties held outside the pale; *Summer of the Danes* with monks sent as delegates on political missions; *The Holy Thief* deals in part with the *Sortes Biblicae*, the use of biblical text to determine messages or make decisions. Theological issues become topics in *The Hermit of Eyton Forest* and *The Heretic's Apprentice* (both deal with the problem of "loose cannons," hermits or heretics). The place of saints in monastic religious experience is a major topic in *A Morbid Taste for Bones, Pilgrim of Hate, Rose Rent, Heretic's Apprentice, The Holy Thief, and Brother Cadfael's Penance*. Above all, the question of genuine vocation may be said to be a question in every novel; it is of primary concern in *A Morbid Taste for Bones, An Excellent Mystery, Brother Cadfael's Penance, Dead Man's Ransom, The Devil's Novice, A Rare Benedictine*, and *The Confession of Brother Haluin*.

The scope of Shrewsbury Abbey's material interests and spiritual responsibilities are representative of the first half of the twelfth century and of Anglo-Norman monasticism, a monasticism that had been revitalized and reformed by the great intellectual and theological leaders from the abbey of Bec, a "house [that] had in a high degree that power—which we call genus loci—of inspiring and molding and bestowing" (Knowles 89). The greatest men of Bec had been Anselm and his pupil, Lanfranc, "who made of Bec for a short while the intellectual centre of Europe north of the Alps" (Knowles 90).

Lanfranc, who had been a lawyer before entering Bec at about the age of thirty-five and who opened a school at the monastery where he taught all comers, became Archbishop of Canterbury (1070-1089); "his was the paramount influence in the monastic world of England" (Knowles 107). He is almost a template for the character of Radulfus; contemporaries described him as possessing "a clarity, an order, a keenness, a granite strength . . . a prudence of the world . . . living kindness . . . benignity and . . . fatherly care with which he ruled his English monks" (Knowles 109).

Lanfranc instituted a number of monastic reforms. Among these was the practice of child oblation—of children given to the monasteries by their parents, who made irrevocable vows on behalf of their children. Benedict had accepted the practice of the *oblati* as one of the two ways of entering conventual life. The other way was that of the *conversi*, which included everyone who entered after boyhood. Most *conversi* were teenagers; adult conversi, such as Lanfranc and Cadfael, were less common. Every conversus was put through a novitiate, usually a year in duration. Then, if he were found acceptable, the novice was permitted to make his final profession. *Oblati* were apparently the norm, *conversi* the exception, during the 1060s through the 1080s. Lanfranc modified the requirements: the *conversi* no longer had to undergo a year-long novitiate, while the *oblati* could make their final vows only when they reached adolescence. Lanfranc began what eventually was "a great change [that] came about by slow and almost imperceptible degrees; the offering of children ceased altogether; the custom of all, or nearly all, proceeding to the priesthood became universal, and the majority of the recruits were either boys sent by their parents without any formal oblation to be educated in the cloister or youths and young men who had received an education at one of the numerous non-monastic schools and (a little later) often also a university training abroad" (Knowles 421). The Cadfael Chronicles take place during this enormous transition.

Cadfael himself is a *conversus* who came late in life; most of his peers were *oblati* or came as children; most of the novices are young men. Cadfael is literate and well educated by life and by training as the herbalist, but he is not a priest; however, young men, such as Mark, have either been ordained or are being educated for ordination.

Cadfael has occasionally been criticized because, having come to his vocation late in life after two careers as soldier and sailor, the monastery appears to be the perfect retirement home. This is to misunderstand Peters's intent. Cadfael is expressive of one of Peters's main themes—that of rich fulfillment of human life on earth as the primary expression of God's love; such fulfillment can occur in either the active life of the husband and father, or in the contemplative life of the monk or nun. Every novel in the series emphasizes Cadfael's deep satisfaction with his life, and it appears almost a superficial spirituality because he is so contented. His is the genuine vocation by which others are measured during the course of these twenty novels, and the issue of the true vocation is perhaps the most significant ongoing theme in the chronicles; at least seven of the novels examine men or women who are called (or think they are called) to this way of life. The majority of these find theirs is not a true call. A few, like Columbanus in *A Morbid Taste for Bones,* are emotionally unstable and ruthlessly ambitious; many, like Brother John in the same novel, have fled to the monastery on the rebound from unhappy love affairs. Instability, ambition and flight by themselves are unacceptable; other candidates come, however, who do not appear at first glance to have a genuine call, yet nevertheless do so: Brother Mark is dropped off by an uncle who does not want him; Ruald is married, rejects his wife in order to take vows and deserts her; Haluin is hounded into the convent by the mother of his beloved. Peters is well aware that vocations do not happen only to people like Cadfael, who enter of their own free will and who have no impediments or responsibilities. Vocations come where God wills. But Peters also notes that such vocations fall within the greater patterns of God's plan and will work out to the greater good.

This begins to seem simplistic, a rather superficial spirituality. Such is not the case. Rather, Peters's vision is that God imbues the world with His spirit, and consequently much of His work is very practical—like Cadfael himself. Cadfael heals (physically and spiritually) where he can, buries where he must, and solves mysteries in order to make healing possible. And he leads an unassuming, quiet spiritual life, praying the Divine Office when he is able and having his own devotion to his personal saint, Saint Winifred. For Cadfael, God appears to be a real but somewhat remote personage; so Cadfael's immediate relationship is with the lady who both is, and is not, in the reliquary at Shrewsbury Abbey, and it is with her that Peters develops "a celebration of medieval mystical Christianity" (Spencer 61). A mystic is a person who has a direct, immediate experience of God. There were many people who described such experiences during the Middle Ages, but a great many more who had personal relationships with the saints. As the poem *Pearl* makes clear, a saved soul is one who has become one with God, and who, therefore, is not only his or her own person but also *is* the deity. Therefore, Winifred is a manifestation of God in a form that Cadfael can understand and with whom he can have a rapport. As a form of God, Winifred has powers of healing and forgiving; she heals Rhun, and she forgives Cadfael when he returns home to Shrewsbury in *Brother Cadfael's Penance*, welcoming him back long before Radulfus does.

The portrait of monastic life that Peters gives her readers in the Cadfael chronicles is that of a healthy institution, of a group of men who are not perfect, but who, by and large, are well-intentioned and faithful to Benedict's vision. They lead lives avoiding the extremes of ascetic spirituality on the one hand and luxurious worldliness on the other. Here is no place for either the monastic mystique nor for seamy sensual or political corruption—and, in fact, Shrewsbury becomes a microcosm reflecting Peters's concept of twelfth-century England as a whole: both Abbey and island are Gardens of Eden, flawed but redeemed, populated by basically good people, some of whom do make tragic mistakes. It is a world that does produce genuine viciousness, but real evil is rare. It can produce chaos, as the civil war between Stephen and Maud testify. But each time sin occurs and chaos threatens to overcome order, God, his saints and his people reassert the pattern of fulfillment. This vision places the monastic life at the very heart of human life, because it is at the heart of God's life. Such was Benedict's vision, and Peters's achievement in these chronicles is gently to reassert the centrality of conventual life to her twentieth-century audience.

Works Cited

Benedict. *The Rule of Saint Benedict.* Trans. and intro. by Cardinal Gasquet. New York: Cooper Square, 1966.

Bouyer, Louis. *A History of Christian Spirituality. The Spirituality of the New Testament and the Fathers.* Vol. 1. New York: Seabury, 1960.

Knowles, Dom David. *The Monastic Order in England: A History of Its Development from the Times of St. Dunstan to the Fourth Lateran Council, 940-1216.* Cambridge: Cambridge UP, 1966.

Spencer, William David. *Mysterium and Mystery: The Clerical Crime Novel.* Ann Arbor: UMI Research, 1989.

Whiteman, Robin. *The Cadfael Companion: The World of Brother Cadfael.* New York: Mysterious P, 1995.

The Moral World of Brother Cadfael

Anthony Hopkins

Ellis Peters's Brother Cadfael is one of the most original detective creations in the past twenty-five years. He is not original because he is entirely new, but because he is new and old both at once, combined of radically innovative elements created entirely by Peters, and of elements deeply reminiscent of previous detectives and previous mystery writers.

Cadfael, as his legions of fans know, is a Welshman who is, in the novels, a Benedictine monk in the Abbey of Saint Peter and Saint Paul in Shrewsbury in Shropshire in England in the twelfth century. A man at arms and crusader before entering the cloister, Cadfael is now the abbey herbalist, and, in consequence, the abbey pharmacist and doctor.

The total of his adventures amounts to twenty. The first of these, *A Morbid Taste for Bones,* takes place in the spring of 1137, with the others following at approximately six-month intervals thereafter. *The Virgin in the Ice,* the sixth Cadfael chronicle, occurs in December 1139. Few mystery series adhere to such a rigidly sequential progress in their detective's careers. Number twenty occurs in 1145.

The murders in these books, in these years, are often associated with political and military developments in one of the more obscure, or at least less popular periods of English history, the years of civil war between the Empress Maud and her rival for the throne, King Stephen. Of their competing claims to rule, Maud's would seem to be the stronger legal case, as she is the daughter of the late king. Stephen, however, has managed to have himself crowned and anointed at a coronation service at Westminster. It is difficult to claim to be more legitimate than an anointed king, but clearly not impossible, since the dual mon-

archs duel for the monarchy throughout the entire period of Cadfael's detective career. Warfare, both military and political, is
often an influential background, sometimes an influential foreground, to the murders, as in *The Virgin in the Ice* and *One
Corpse Too Many,* which takes place mainly after a successful
siege of Shrewsbury.

A major consequence of this choice of an unknown historical period is that Peters, her characters, and her audience move
in a world about which we have no preconceptions. This is not
the world of Henry VIII, Elizabeth I, Cromwell or Victoria, English periods which we know, or feel we know, something about.
This is a new historical world, almost a Neverland, with its own
rules, its own laws, its own identity, within which we are always,
by comparison with our familiarity with the more famous days
of England's glory, always novices, always strangers. And it is a
borderland, with Shropshire at the far western edge of England,
almost beyond the law, next to the lawless, or at least disobedient
paradise of Wales just next door.

It is also a very rural world. The detective novel, as a rule,
is aggressively urban in nature. The detectives—such as Holmes
or Marlowe or Poirot—live in cities. Their clients are city, or
city-style people; the murders take place, frequently, indoors.
Even the Agatha Christie country house is filled for the weekend
by persons down from the city. Nevertheless, Cadfael's is a
world where people travel. Not often great distances, for a day's
travel by foot or by mule, even by horse, is risibly small compared to the miles we can cover on our way to Florida in a day.
The geographical area of a Peters's mystery is quite small. But
still, it is a world of surprising mobility, more reminiscent of car
travel by freeway and highway than the searching of the drawing
room and library and garden of the manor.

Peters, even though Cadfael's abbey is just outside the city
walls, takes us to an outdoor, agricultural world. Her Cadfael
novels are filled with the rhythms of the seasons: the rains of
spring, summer heat, the rich harvests of the cooling autumns,
the snows of December. Murders often take place out of doors in
fields and in forests. Cadfael lives for his garden, lives sur-
rounded by flourishing fragrance and color:

He used the respite to walk the length of his pale flowered, fragrant inner kingdom. . . .

Glossy and dim, oiled and furry, the leaves tendered every possible variation of green. The flowers were mostly shy, small, almost furtive, in soft sidelong colours, lilacs and shadowy blues and diminutive yellows. . . .

Rue, sage, rosemary, gilvers, gromwell, ginger, mint thyme, columbine, herb of grace, savoury, mustard, every manner of herb grew here, fennel, tansy, basil and dill, parsley, chervil, and marjoram. . . .

His herbs called attention to themselves only by their disseminated sweetness as the sun rose. (*Bones* 8)

It is a world that is realized and brought to life not so much by the completeness with which Peters presents and describes it, but by the naturalness that informs her descriptions of that world. In general, she does not explain every vocabulary term, she does not give definitions or laborious contextualizations. What she does seem to do is to imagine the medieval world totally in her mind, then write about those parts of it she needs to use as if the reader already knows that world. So, for example, the beginning of *A Morbid Taste for Bones* identifies, but does not fulsomely describe, the functions and business of a monastic day:

This third Mass of the day was non-parochial and brief, and after it the Benedictine brothers of the abbey of Shrewsbury filed in procession from the choir into the chapter-house, and made their way to their stalls in due order. (6)

Similarly, the description below surrounds the reader with many terms, but only a few tentative definitions. As a result, the reader must interpret, figure out, from the context, the likely meaning of words, thereby creating the medieval world for themselves as they read:

[T]he oxen leaned into their yokes and heaved, and the ploughman behind them clung and dragged at the heavy share. Before the leading pair a man walked backwards, arms gently waving and beckoning, his goad only a wand, flourished for magic, not for its sting, his high, pure calls carried aloft on the air, cajoling and praising. Towards him the beasts leaned willingly, following his cries with all their might. The new-turned soil, greyish-brown and sluggish, heaved moist and fresh to light after the share. (*Bones* 24)

As a kind of footnote to the authenticity of the medieval world Peters creates, there is one continuing feature of this world that seems inauthentic, or, at least, unconvincing. Peters has a special fondness for fifty-year-old men. They are often presented as pre-eminent in social and political and family affairs, as a combination of energy, experience, judgment and power that makes them quite formidable. The pattern for these men is set by the first of them, Rhisiart in *A Morbid Taste for Bones:*

Rhisiart was a big, bluff hearty-looking man of about fifty, high-coloured and dark-haired, with a short grizzled beard, and bold features that could be merry or choleric, fierce or jovial, but were far too expressive to be secretive or mean. (45)

Rhisiart, of course, is the murder victim in this novel. His power, his energy, his influence in the community stand in the way of the transfer of Saint Winifred to Shrewsbury, so he has to go—as do, in the later novels, many other fifty-year-old men.

Men in their prime are not the only victims Peters creates and kills, but there are enough of them to notice. However, having men in their prime being represented as being fifty strikes me as a very modern conceptualization of age. In the twelfth century, fifty was not the age of people in their prime, fifty was the age of people who were dead. Often long dead.

People did not live long in the middle ages. They matured quickly. Boys went to university at fifteen. They married young, they dropped from petty diseases, from injuries that turned quickly septic, from untreatable internal illnesses, from exposure, from the very medical treatments intended to cure them. A common response to medicinal bleeding that seemed not to be effective was to bleed the patient again. In the twelfth century, fifty would be very old indeed, and by making the curve of aging in Cadfael's world essentially similar to our own, Peters distorts her medieval accuracy to accommodate the tastes and expectations of a contemporary audience, who would feel, if the third age started at forty, that they were all always on the wrong side of the mountain entrance to Shangri-La.

Moving backwards in time legitimizes a kind of moving back psychologically. There are no Freudian neurotics in the middle ages, there are no group therapy sessions, there are no unresolved Oedipal conflicts. There are only interesting characters hell-bent on having their own way no matter what. There is, in plenty, in Cadfael's world, raw, old-fashioned emotion and passion—jealousy, greed, envy, lust, revenge, avarice, hatred—clear, direct motives for direct, even if hidden action.

But primarily, the most significant consequence of the movement back in time is that there is no forensic science or investigative technology. No post-mortems, no DNA testing, no fingerprints, no chemical analyses, no blood typing—none of the paraphernalia of modernity that always takes all the fun out of figuring out who done it, that always threatens to overwhelm the real detective skills and faculties—observation, intuition, intelligence, and reason.

In contemporary detection, science is often a great inconvenience, as it threatens to solve the mystery without the help of the detective. And then where would we be? Throughout Agatha Christie, and P. D. James, and Ruth Rendell there are a host of strategies—such as the isolation in a country house in a rainstorm—to keep police expertise in general, and scientific expertise in particular, at bay.

But in Cadfael there is no police expertise, for there are no police, and certainly no science, so that Cadfael has the luxury of classic detective investigation—"pure" detective work, if you like—observation of evidence at the scene and careful questioning of witnesses and suspects. The detective detects, and the outcome of the mystery is directly the consequence of the detective's mind working on the problem. I stress this because, to me, this is the cornerstone of the mystery genre—the solution of a major problem by the application of a single mind to that problem.

It is a stroke of genius, not for Peters to make Cadfael a monk, but to make him a monk who is able to be a good detective, and to achieve that, Peters takes this new idea—that the detective is a monk, and welds it to an old idea—that the detective is a life-hardened loner. The best short description of Cadfael comes from Peters's *A Rare Benedictine*, a trio of short stories which show a Cadfael younger than the fifty-seven-year-old of the first novel. In 1120, still a soldier, but just before he enters the abbey, Peters describes Cadfael as:

[T]he Welsh man-at-arms, blunt and insubordinate as he was, was also experienced and accomplished in arms, a man of his word, once given, and utterly reliable in whatever situation on land or sea, for in both elements he had long practice behind him. (12)

That seems a description largely applicable to Philip Marlowe. I do not suggest that Peters has plagiarized. It does seem to me, though, that part of Cadfael's originality is that he is rather less like British detectives and rather more like an American one. Both Marlowe and Cadfael have had previous careers as policeman and soldier respectively. Both have been battered and wearied by the world, both have rather low expectations of human perfection. Both are largely celibate, although experienced in mature relationships. Both have close ties with the cops, both are marginal to normal society. Neither is a genius, although both are intelligent. Neither is ambitious, both are doggedly loyal to the task and to an honor-girded professionalism. The big difference, of course, is that Marlowe is cynical and hard-boiled, while Cadfael is tolerant and generous and forgiving of human weakness.

At any rate, it is clear that Cadfael is not of a religious temperament. He is not driven to prayer, contemplation, and the perfection of the soul. He is an old soldier come to a safe haven, and it is almost always his background in the world that gives him the knowledge and experience to find the killer. Peters, in fact, tends slightly to disparage professional ecclesiastics, for they know nothing but God, and have little wisdom to bring to His service. Cadfael, however, of whom she surely approves, regularly lies, cheats, and steals. At the end of *The Virgin in the Ice* he arranges for Olivier, who is on the enemy side, to escape. In *A Morbid Taste for Bones* he steals the relic of the saint's skeleton, substitutes the body of a dead man, frightens a murderer into confession by having someone impersonate the ghost of the dead saint, fakes a miracle using the habit of a dead monk, and, in passing, condones murder because the victim probably deserved killing anyway:

> "You dared, you dared touch her," blazed Engelard in towering rage. "You worthless cloister rat!" And he took Columbanus by the throat and hoisted him bodily from the ground, shook him like the rat he had called him, cracked him in the air like a poisonous snake, and when he had done with him, flung him down at his feet in the grass. (172)
> "He can't be dead." . . . "I barely handled him at all." (173)

This, if not murder, is certainly manslaughter, but because Cadfael is a good man, and his deceptions are rendered in a good cause, obviously everything is all O.K. I might note here that Sherlock Holmes lets the occasional murderer go free if the perpetrator has killed a particularly nasty person. One of the many comforts of the mystery form is that as long as you are a good person, you can do as much bad as you can get away with.

Yet, on the other hand, Cadfael is always a reliable spiritual advisor. In *Virgin in the Ice,* for example, he counsels:

> "[Y]ou may not take to yourself the guilt of the evil another has done." (178)

> [S]urely our little faults do not deserve so crushing a penalty. Without time to reconsider, to repent, to make reparation. Youth destroyed by folly when youth should be allowed its follies on the way to maturity and sense. (57)

Cadfael is such a good man that even his sinning is righteous. We all need friends just like that—worldly, kind, trustworthy and faithful.

The social world of Cadfael is one of the more successful of the medieval aspects of Peters's work. Nowhere does she describe all the structural intricacies of the feudal system, but they are everywhere present in the novels and in just about every social encounter. It is a world, both in the abbey and out, that is everywhere hierarchical, where the hierarchy is infinitely graded and aligned in complex, interlocking ways, where protocol, deference, manners are everywhere judged and everywhere used and—thoroughly known to all. This order is reflected in clothing, jewels, houses, position at table, position in church. It is a world based on and sustained by a known, formal order.

Yet, the background of many novels is social chaos—civil war in which barons change sides more often than they change their clothing, where, with regularity, cities are sacked, religious houses despoiled, where, in *The Virgin in the Ice,* a robber sets up as a free-lance overlord—his own independent band of outlaws, his own castle, his own power his only allegiance—the complete negation of the ordered medieval ideal. This continuing contrast between ideal social order and political chaos gives almost every novel a constant moral tension, and a wider social frame of reference than is usual in the mystery genre.

Usually, in a medieval atmosphere, the social realms are restricted to two—the nobility and the peasantry. In Cadfael, the social norm is the middle class—master craftsmen, priests, landholders, minor nobility, merchants and traders. Quite absent are dukes, earls, counts, princes. Even Cadfael's friend, Hugh Beringar, is the deputy, not the High Sheriff. It is not that the higher nobility are entirely absent from the novels, it is that they are seldom the driving force of plot, problem, or resolution.

In emphasizing the middle class, Peters at once innovates by departing from the conventional ways of portraying medieval society, and repeats by emphasizing the traditionally normal and the traditionally moral class of both mystery characters and mystery readers. The mystery audience, I believe, is the managerial class—people of education and responsibility, but not of exceptional wealth or power. Certainly I believe that it is the values of this class which dominate the mystery form—the class that always has to solve problems, that always has to solve everyone else's problems.

Also innovative, in Peters's case, is her successful, in my view, attempt to bring the mystery form closer and closer to the shape and interest of a real novel, where character and moral outcome dominate, and where plot is driven by emotional, not murderous, impulses. Whereas detective fiction habitually contains one plot, one story only, or, at best, combines the main story of the murder with a minor substory, Peters weaves together three distinct, yet intertwined stories, and only one of these is directly the story of the murder as such. In *A Morbid Taste for Bones,* for example, the initial story is that of rescuing the bones of the saint from their church in Wales and taking them off to the abbey in Shrewsbury. Religious motives, to put it generously, drive this action, and drive it from beginning to end. Then there is the story of the young lovers, a story exacerbated by the murder, but a story with its own integrity and moral difficulties both before and after the murder takes place, before and after it is solved. Finally, there is the story of the murder, the motive and action to be discovered and brought to light so that murder may be exposed. Each of these three gets equal time within the book, each is given equal legitimacy within the book. Peters takes these three, makes each dependent on the other, but never loses sight of any. At the end of the novel, all are resolved, yet each is resolved in its own terms.

The moral behavior that Ellis Peters allows her characters to go through indicates that the moral world of Brother Cadfael is a very complicated, tense, sometimes self-contradictory one. The description of Cadfael as someone utterly reliable, but who lies, cheats, and steals, suggests the moral spectrum possible in medieval England.

The general orientation of the mystery genre, in terms of morality, is, I feel, the general secular sense that the world is in a state, fundamentally, of order. Murder destroys that order, solving the murder restores order, restores the world to its normally ordered condition.

Cadfael's moral world, perhaps because it is a world created within a thoroughly Christian framework, tends to present a fallen world in fundamental disorder. Think of the levels of chaos, confusion, imperfection, that can be traced so easily in the novels. There is no secure foundation to the state or for government of any kind. It is less than a hundred years since the Norman conquest, and the question of succession has not been solved. Two different people claim the throne, and are willing, both, to press that claim by violence. This is not civil war by rebellion, by the downtrodden uprising against their unworthy betters. This is self-centred and deliberate lawlessness on the part of those whose duty it is to offer protection to the nation.

Since this is medieval warfare, one should perhaps not be surprised that victory is followed by looting and reprisal, but on more than one occasion this involves the destruction of churches and the despoilation of religious houses. In *One Corpse Too Many*, for example, the evil of civil war has come to Shrewsbury with the attack on and capture of the city, followed by the execution of almost a hundred turncoats. This is par for the course of medieval warfare, however. Only when one extra person is killed for private motives does anyone, including Cadfael, think in terms of crime. In *Virgin in the Ice* bands of outlaws can substantially challenge civil authority. For a world in which honour of person, of family, is paramount, loyalty seems a quality in very short supply. In more than one novel Cadfael and Hugh Beringar talk at the beginning, bringing each other and the readers up to date on the doings of the war, and as often as they talk about battles lost and won, they talk about which list of barons has changed sides for the occasion—again. It is a world in which a man's word is his bond, but in which no one likes the discipline of bondage.

Against this childishness of their leaders and rulers, conventional citizens are, if not all but helpless, certainly not fully in control of their lives.

The moral leaders of this world are in total confusion, but when Peters moves down the social scale she scarcely moves up the moral scale. The middle classes are not significantly more moral than the nobles. It is within this middle class that Peters typically finds her murders—the victims, the murderers, and the motives—usually motives of lust and greed, and usually motives that require the betrayal of a friend, subordinate, or superior. In *A Morbid Taste for Bones* the murderer kills his patron and protector, and a monk murders in the name of God. In *The Virgin in the Ice*, a young son to a minor noble murders a nun. When asked if the killer will hang, the sheriff says, "I doubt it" (270).

Within the cloister the monks tend to be presented as human rather than holy, having human, rather than spiritual weaknesses. Such an approach is hardly an exercise in anticlerical exposure of lapses from perfection, but it does suggest that

Peters does not develop the religious or contemplative aspects of monastic life.

Although it is a Christian world, it is a world that contains habits and practices that we would find deeply offensive, perhaps even unbelievable. One such practice, of course, is villeinage. Peasants are, essentially, so dependent on their lords that they are, in effect, owned by them. It is a period in which oblation—the giving of extremely small children to the church—is practiced. There are always small groups of 8-9-10-year-old novices running around the abbey. It is a world in which kidnap, followed by rape, is the prelude to enforced marriage—which then cannot be dissolved.

Prior Robert, in *A Morbid Taste for Bones,* not to put too fine a point on it, offers a bribe to Rhisiart to let the saint's relics go permanently to Shrewsbury. It is also a monk who murders in this novel, which also condones another murder because the victim pretty well deserved to die anyway.

Additionally, in many of the chronicles, there is a kind of free-lance *ad hoc* creation of moral standards by the hero. As long as Cadfael is true to the murder victim, he can pretty much do whatever he likes. It is not Winifred's bones, for example, which go to the abbey.

This thoroughly corrupted world echoes the world of the American hard-boiled school in which, as the novel progresses, more and more levels of increasing and increasingly powerful forms of corruption become uncovered. It is not that no one is good, but that the good, such as sheriffs and abbots, are few and far between, and their goodness tends to centre on a few ethical standards they will not compromise. All the rest is up for grabs.

So where is there, if at all, moral order in Cadfael's world? Given its totally fallen state, simply solving the murder hardly counts as an act of moral decisiveness. We find in Cadfael a kind of moral order in the seasons—the cycle of renewal that overrides and ignores human politics and human imperfection, and a genuine moral order in the sense of God's presence, not in miracles, and not, often, in moral behavior, but in moral achievements such as Christmas, such as marriage, such as the (potential) reconciliation of father and son when Cadfael discovers that Olivier is his son. Illustrative of the definition of moral force that Peters creates is her quite charming obsession with young love. In novel after novel there will be emphatic attention paid to one or two young couples against whom are ranged a panoply of great impediments of class, fortune, father, economic disparity. Sometimes such couples are deeply involved in the circumstances of the murder, sometimes not, but one of Peters's main goals seems to be to ensure that young people will escape victoriously together, if not into marriage, at least over the border to the safety of Wales. In *Virgin in the Ice* this couple is Ermina and Olivier. In *A Morbid Taste for Bones,* there are two—Sioned and Engelard, and Annest and (Brother) John.

In dealing with such people, Peters is always on the feminist side of sexual equality. The young men are presented, usually, as just a little bit stupid. Whatever young women may be looking for in men, a domineering intelligence seems not at the top of the list of basic requirements. Over and over the young women are presented as vibrant, vivid, energetic and commanding. In fact, Peters's ability to create convincing descriptions of dynamic young women is one of her unique achievements as a mystery writer. For example, here is Sioned of Wales:

She might have been eighteen or nineteen years old, possibly younger, for there was a certain erect assurance about her that gave her the dignity of maturity even though she had just dropped out of an oak tree. And for all her bare feet and mane of unbraided dark hair, she was no villein girl. Everything about her said clearly that she knew her worth. Her gown was of fine homespun wool, dyed a soft blue, and had embroidery at neck and sleeves.

No question but she was a beauty. Her face was oval and firm of feature, the hair that fell in wild waves was almost black with a tint of dark and brilliant red in it where the light caught, and the large black-lashed eyes that considered Brother Cadfael with such frank interest were of almost the same colour, dark as damsons, bright as the sparkles of mica in the river pebbles. (*Bones* 34)

Then there is Ermina from *The Virgin in the Ice:*

The girl's hood had fallen back on her neck, the red light flowed over a great disordered coil of dark hair, a wide clear forehead, arched imperious black brows, large eyes too brilliant to be black, by the reflections in them the darkest and reddest of browns. She had, for all her coarse country clothes, a carriage of the head and a lance-like directness of gaze that queens might have copied. The lines that swooped so graciously over her cheekbones and down to full strongly folded lips and resolute chin made so suave a moulding that Cadfael's finger ends, once accomplished in such caresses, stroked down from brow to throat in imagination, and quivered to old memories. (123)

This emphasis on the young, the emphasis on young women, the bond between the young women and the older, gentle warrior Cadfael, the emphasis on rule breaking, the emphasis on the natural, victorious rhythms of the seasons, the developing emphasis, as the series progresses, on the intensified search for recognition between father and son, these, more than the solution of the murders, signify, finally, that Cadfael's is an ordered, moral world. But the order is the dynamic, fruitful order of forces more natural, more powerful, than flawed human social and political constructs. It is, in some form, a supernatural order whose emblems of love, marriage, birth, forgiveness and reunification echo the promise of a Christian heaven.

Such terms, perhaps, are rarely applied to a murder mystery, a whodunit, a form whose sense of moral order usually does not get much beyond the notion that murder is bad; solving murder is good.

Part of the surprise comes from a sense of formal liberation from concentration on one story only, liberation from concentration on the murder to allow the presentation of two or three interlocking stories simultaneously, particularly the arrangement of a primary story and then the story of the murder which is dependent on the first. This expansion and reconfiguration literally doubles the aesthetic range of the mystery as an art form, moving it towards being truly a novel and away from the limitations of formula fiction.

Primarily, however, there is liberation from the simple-minded morals framework of the conventional detective story into a morally complicated, fundamentally imperfect world, including the opportunity for the solution to the murder to be associated not just with a return to order, but with an enhancement of order and harmony, as in the ending to *The Virgin in the Ice:*

Cadfael rode mute and content, still full of the wonder and astonishment, all elation and all humility. Eleven more days to the Christmas feast, and no shadow hanging over it now, only a great light. A time of births, of triumphant begettings, and this year how richly celebrated— the son of the young woman from Worcester, the son of Aline and Hugh, the son of Mariam, the son of Man.

A son to be proud of! Yes, amen! (271)

Works Cited

Peters, Ellis. *A Morbid Taste for Bones*. 1977. London: Warner, 1992.
——. *One Corpse Too Many*. 1979. London: Futura, 1984.
——. *A Rare Benedictine*. 1988. London: Headline, 1990.
——. *The Virgin in the Ice*. 1982. London: Warner Futura, 1992.

Fathers in the Chronicles of Brother Cadfael

Carol A. Mylod

A most intriguing element in Ellis Peters's Cadfael Chronicles is the portrayal of fatherhood. Reflections of the medieval world abound in the exploration of this relationship, e.g., depictions of occupations, attitudes, customs, laws, and religious beliefs.

Then as now, a good father protects, supports, nourishes, disciplines, defends, nurtures, understands, loves, and, in some circumstances, is willing to lay down his life for his child. Men can be fathers in the biological sense of engendering children, in the psychological sense of encouraging young people toward self-knowledge and maturity, in the spiritual sense of fostering religious development, and in the political sense of protecting and leading the citizenry.

Among the ongoing characters in the series, the central character, Brother Cadfael, and two of his closest friends and allies, Sheriff Hugh Beringar and Abbot Radulfus, are particularly admirable fathers. Less frequently featured series characters like Owain, Prince of Gwynedd, and Brother Paul, Master of Novices, are also good fathers. By contrast, series characters like Prior Robert and Brother Jerome largely fail in their obligations as fathers. So does King Stephen as he vies with Empress Maud for the throne and ineptly leads England through a period of bloody civil war.

While managing the Abbey herb garden, doctoring the sick, and ferreting out murderers, Brother Cadfael is a spiritual, a psychological, and even a biological father. Cadfael does not find out until he is sixty in the sixth book of the series, *The Virgin in the Ice,* that he is the father of a splendid son, Olivier de Bretagne.

Olivier's mother was Mariam, a Syrian widow from Antioch, whom ex-crusader Cadfael had known and loved during his sea-faring days before he entered the Benedictines at age forty. Absolutely stunned by the news and believing that he has received the greatest gift of his lifetime, Cadfael echoes the "Nunc Dimittis" prayed by the holy man, Simeon, after experiencing his own greatest blessing: beholding the child Jesus in the temple at the time of His presentation (*Virgin* 197-98).

In a narrow sense of fatherhood, Cadfael fosters religious development by training a whole series of raw novices in the ways of the Benedictine Rule as they help him in the herb garden. Brothers John, Mark, Oswin, and Winfrid come to mind. In a wider sense, Cadfael encourages moral development in the course of his detecting by recalling sinners, some of them murderers, to repentance, confession, and atonement. Cadfael is also spiritual father to his godchild, Giles, holy-terror son of Hugh and Aline Beringar. This spiritual obligation is regarded so seriously that Cadfael is given great freedom from monastic duties to attend to Giles.

Throughout the Chronicles, a whole series of likable young people cross Cadfael's path during their perilous adventures. Being inordinately fond of and sympathetic to young people, Cadfael feeds, hides, comforts, defends, counsels, disguises, and abets these young people. He protects them from rival political forces, unhappy marriages, greedy relatives, unsympathetic parents, ill-conceived vocations, hypocritical clergy, brutal masters, and even potential murderers. In these grand mystery stories, the young people grow up (the girls faster than the boys according to psychological father Cadfael). In the best tradition of the comedy of manners, the young people frequently find happiness in marriage.

Introduced in the second chronicle, *One Corpse Too Many,* when King Stephen appoints him deputy sheriff, Hugh Beringar is a biological father to the aforementioned young Giles and a political father to the county of Shropshire, which is staunchly loyal to Stephen. Hugh comes into even greater responsibility when he succeeds the murdered Gilbert Prestcote as sheriff of the shire in the ninth chronicle, *Dead Man's Ransom.* Shropshire under Hugh has the reputation for being the best governed shire in the country. Hugh sees his job as upholding the King's justice and keeping the King's peace—not an easy task amid the anarchy of civil war.

Hugh aims to preserve life and property. To that end, he comes up against a whole series of formidable adversaries: the outlaw leader Alain le Gaucher holed up with his masterless men atop Titterstone Clee in *The Virgin in the Ice,* the renegade Earl of Essex, Geoffrey de Manderville, behind his impenetrable fortress in the Fen country in *The Potter's Field,* the invading Welshmen of Powys led by Madog ap Meredith in *Dead Man's Ransom,* as well as the forces of Empress Maud massed against King Stephen during the battle of Lincoln. Hugh's command suffers the fewest possible casualties because of its meticulous training, fine equipment, and skilled leadership.

Hugh Beringar keeps a watchful eye on those self-seeking half brothers to the north, the Earls of Chester and Lincoln, ostensibly loyal to Stephen, who seek any opportunity to increase their holdings. Hugh also has a good working relationship with Robert, Earl of Leicester, to the south (*The Holy Thief*) and Owain, Prince of Gywnedd, to the west (*Dead Man's Ransom* and *The Summer of the Danes*).

As Sheriff of Shropshire in charge of the garrison and the jail at Shrewsbury Castle, Hugh is involved whenever a crime is committed. With the force of law and civil authority behind him, he does much of the leg work and investigating when his good friend Cadfael is embroiled in a baffling murder.

Introduced in the third chronicle, *Monk's-Hood,* when he replaces the saintly Abbot Heribert, Abbot Radulfus is a spiritual and psychological father. As abbot of the Benedictine foundation of Saint Peter and Saint Paul in Shrewsbury, he is responsible for its inhabitants: monks, novices, school boys, lay servants, and visiting guests. Abbot Radulfus is also responsible for Benedictines from Shrewsbury who live and work outside the Abbey, e.g., at the leper hospital at Saint Giles or the sheepfold at Rhydycroesau near the Welsh border, as well as visiting Benedictines from sister houses like Hyde Mead (Brother Humilis and Brother Fidelis in *An Excellent Mystery*) or Ramsey (Brother Sulien in *The Potter's Field* and Brothers Herluin and Tutilo in *The Holy Thief*). Radulfus regards his wardship of young Richard Ludel (*The Hermit of Eyton Forest*) as a sacred trust.

Radulfus's religious court has jurisdiction if a crime is committed on Benedictine property or by a monk who has taken, at the very least, minor orders. Radulfus is also the guardian of Abbey privilege against encroachment by town officials, e.g., the revenues engendered by Saint Peter's Fair. Radulfus is an austere man of great wisdom, deep integrity, subtle sensitivity, fine organizational skills, and wry humor. Peters wrote admiringly about Radulfus: "The honor and integrity of his house was his prime concern and in that criterion pure justice was implied" (*Leper* 94).

Cadfael, Hugh, and Radulfus admire each other's character, appreciate each other's skills and experience, respect each other's intelligence, and trust each other's judgment. As the central character in the series, Cadfael acts as the "agent of justice" (*Benedictine* 3). Radulfus and Hugh speak for heavenly and earthly justice respectively. Besides being good friends, all three men share the quality of being able to overlook something if justice will be better served. When these three men gather in Radulfus's parlor to plan strategy or to review the outcome of a murder investigation, the reader knows that all will be well.

A minor character in the series referred to often but featured extensively only in *Dead Man's Ransom* and *The Summer of the Danes,* Owain Gwynedd is a kind, loving, forgiving father to his family and an ideal ruler for his Welsh people. He acknowledges his illegitimate son, Hywel, treats him with honor and respect according to Welsh law, and gives him a position of authority. Owain forgives his kinsman, Elis ap Cynan, whom he had lovingly placed in fosterage, for going on an ill-fated raid into Shropshire with Madog and his men of Powys and then getting caught by a bunch of nuns.

Owain does not demand his brother Cadwaladyr's life when Cadwaladyr arranges for the murder of the prince of Deheubarth but, rather, exiles him from his lands. When Cadwaladyr traitorously entices Otir and his Irish Danes into Wales with promises of booty and money if they will fight against Owain to regain the confiscated lands, Owain does his utmost not to shed the blood of one Welsh subject because of Cadwaladyr's self-serving folly.

Owain proclaims that Cadwaladyr will not get from him "a coin spent" or "a man put at risk" (*Danes* 156). With his severely tested forbearance and his restraint, Owain Gwynedd plays the forgiving father again and again to Cadwaladyr's prodigal son, and, at the same time, spares his people the harsh realities of war.

Another minor character in the series, Brother Paul, kindly, patient, scholarly, and indulgent, bears mentioning as a good father. As master of novices, he is also in charge of the school-boys, some of whom are very young, easily intimidated, and extremely homesick. He teaches, encourages, loves, and protects his young charges, novices and schoolboys alike, always standing between them and harsh treatment or excessive discipline for minor infractions.

Novice Meriet Aspley in *The Devil's Novice* and ten-year-old schoolboy Richard Ludel in *The Hermit of Eyton Forest* particularly benefit from Paul's loving care. Meriet is saved from an unsought religious vocation thrust upon him by his father and Richard is spared marriage to a much older woman arranged by his grandmother in order to consolidate estates.

As second in command to Abbot Radulfus, the aristocratic Prior Robert should possess many qualities of a good father. He does not. Instead, he is a reasonably competent administrator always dancing attendance on anyone of importance. While Radulfus's passion is God's justice and mercy, the arrogant Robert seems incapable of passion except when advancing his own career. His main concern is that nothing upset the surface serenity of the Abbey's day. Robert lacks any real regard for others. In his role as spiritual father, he is preoccupied with the letter of the law rather than its spirit. When Brother John escapes his clutches by remaining in Wales to marry the beautiful Annest rather than coming back to continue his novitiate at Shrewsbury Abbey, Peters wrote that "Prior Robert's Norman spirit burned at being deprived of his rightful victim" (*Bones* 224).

As Prior Robert's assistant, the hypocritical Brother Jerome does Robert's dirty work. He eavesdrops, meddles, spies on people, and carries tales (frequently with incorrect information) back to Prior Robert, so Robert can preserve the illusion of being above such unworthy activities.

Jerome becomes more sinful as the series progresses. Jerome's obvious spite, cowardly mean-spiritedness, and gross lack of charity are particularly reprehensible because he is a priest. Jerome is chaplain and confessor to the novices and schoolboys who usually go in the opposite direction when they see him coming—a sad commentary on his character. In *The Holy Thief,* Jerome descends to a new low when he attempts to murder Brother Tutilo. Fortunately, he cannot even get that right.

King Stephen is a poor father to his people because he has not been able to protect them from the anarchy of civil war—men killed, women raped, children loose on the roads, animals slaughtered, crops and manors burned, property stolen, monasteries looted, and masterless men roving in outlaw bands.

Although personally brave, generous, and charming, Stephen lacks the qualities of a good general, particularly the persistence to make a plan and see it through as well as the perspicacity to follow up an advantage. He becomes bored easily and abandons a successful siege or, with more chivalry than common sense, allows an enemy to escape, thus prolonging the war. In *The Confession of Brother Haluin,* Peters suggested that Stephen allows Empress Maud to escape his siege of Oxford because he does not know what to do with her if he captures her (6). Cadfael wryly observes that "surely there never had been such a king as Stephen for conjuring defeat out of victory" (*Confession* 7).

Lacking a strong, well-disciplined character, Stephen is too easily influenced by others. In *One Corpse Too Many,* he slaughters the survivors of the fallen Shrewsbury Castle garrison and then instantly regrets it. Realizing that as a ruler Empress Maud is no better than King Stephen, Cadfael comments shrewdly: "There's little to choose between two such monarchs" (*Corpse* 11).

Examples of good and bad fathers also present themselves in the individual books of the Brother Cadfael series. The good fathers seem to serve more as protectors and supporters of their charges while the poor fathers, more often than not, serve as catalysts for tragic action.

Good fathers want their daughters happily settled so they accept their choice of husband. For example, Welsh lord, Tudur ap Rhys (*Ransom*) dissolves a long-standing, solemnly binding betrothal contract so that his daughter Christina can marry Eluid ap Griffith, the man of her choice. For the sake of his daughter Annet, Eilmund, the forester, (*Hermit*) hides the escaped villein Hyacinth who hopes to become free by remaining in a charter borough like Shrewsbury for a year and a day. Wealthy wool merchant, Girard of Lythwood (*Apprentice*), extends his protection and support to Elave, a young man wrongly accused of heresy and murder, who is beloved by Girard's foster daughter Fortunata. All three romances supported by understanding fathers result in happy marriages.

Additionally, seventy-year-old ex-crusader, Guimar de Massard (*Leper*), maimed by leprosy, takes eight years to walk home from the Holy Land to be sure his orphaned granddaughter Iveta inherits her lands. His intervention results in Iveta's marriage to the young squire, Joscelin de Lucy, instead of to the gross, old baron, Huon de Domville, who was mainly interested in Iveta for her great wealth.

Good fathers support and defend sons who get into trouble while sowing some wild oats. For example, abbey steward, William Rede (*Benedictine*), excuses his son's brawling, gambling, and debts by saying that he is no worse than any other young man his age. Eddi Rede repays his father's support by helping to catch the man who attempted William's murder. Master shoemaker and Provost of Shrewsbury, Geoffrey Corviser (*Fair*), stands by his son Philip who is charged with drunkenness, inciting to riot, and murder. Corviser's faith in his son is proven to be justified.

Good fathers listen to and protect their charges. Welsh lord Rhisiart (*Bones*) will not surrender Saint Winifred's bones according to his own conviction and the wishes of his people just because some Benedictines at the Abbey of Saint Peter and Saint Paul want to remove the bones from Wales to Shrewsbury where the relics would become a significant draw for pilgrims, and, thus, a source of considerable income.

When bad fathers put their own needs, desires, and ambitions ahead of their children's, murder is frequently the result. In *Monk's-Hood*, cantankerous, argumentative Gervase Bonel, the lord of a small manor, does not provide fairly for his illegitimate son and only offspring, Meurig, who is driven to poison his father. In *The Sanctuary Sparrow,* wealthy but greedy goldsmith Walter Aurifaber works his daughter Susanna like a slave and does not provide a dowry so that she can make an honorable marriage. When she steals from her father, murders the man who threatens to reveal her crime, and takes flight to Wales with her lover, she and her unborn child are killed by pursuing soldiers.

Some poor fathers are perfectly willing to dump children who may prove embarrassing into religious foundations. For example, in the mistaken idea that his son Meriet is a murderer and in an attempt to save the family public disgrace, Leoric Aspley (*Novice*) insists that his son enter the Benedictines—with disastrous results. Additionally, Canon Meirion (*Danes*) finds the presence of his daughter Heledd a hindrance to his ambitious plan to rise in the newly Romanized Welsh church so he plots to hide her away in an English convent. Heledd, one of the most interesting and finely drawn characters in a series filled with strong, attractive women, takes matters into her own hands by eloping to Ireland with Turcaill, one of the invaders from the Danish kingdom of Dublin.

Other bad fathers like parish priest Father Ailnoth (*Raven*) place the pursuit of personal perfection ahead of ministering to souls. Ailnoth chooses to fulfill the requirement to say his office rather than to baptize a dying child to whom he later refuses Christian burial.

Throughout the series, the three most important good fathers, Brother Cadfael, Sheriff Hugh, and Abbot Radulfus, are frequently compared to the Biblical ideal of fatherhood, the Good Shepherd, who would lay down his life for his sheep and who is a figure for the Heavenly Father. The Good Shepherd is a particularly apt metaphor for this series because sheep and the wool trade were the foundations of wealth in medieval Shrewsbury.

Cadfael, Hugh, and Radulfus certainly think and speak in the Biblical language of the Good Shepherd. In *The Virgin in the Ice,* Cadfael thinks about the body of Sister Hilaria, raped and murdered and frozen in the ice: "A lamb, after all, a lost ewe-lamb, a lamb of God, stripped and violated and slaughtered" (36). In *Brother Cadfael's Penance,* citing his duty to look for his son Olivier, lost in the aftermath of a major struggle between King Stephen and Empress Maud, Cadfael seeks permission from Radulfus to go to a peace conference at Coventry, but says that he must go, with or without permission. Radulfus gives him leave to go, saying that " 'it is my office to keep all my flock. If one strays, the ninety and nine left are also bereft' " (17). Also in *Brother Cadfael's Penance*, Sheriff Hugh explains to Earl Robert of Leicester that he is trying to keep his people of Shropshire alive and whole during the chaos of civil war. He says: " 'I had better be about shepherding my own flock' " (181).

Like the ideal of the Good Shepherd, Cadfael, Hugh, and Radulfus put their lives on the line in many instances in the series. In *A Morbid Taste for Bones*, Cadfael lunges at Columbanus as he tries to stab Sioned with a dagger after she unmasks his hypocritical pose as a receiver of visions from Saint Winifred. In *The Pilgrim of Hate*, again unarmed and this time outnumbered, Cadfael wades into a melee to prevent the evil thief and murderer, Simon Poer, from killing Brother Matthew. In *Monk's-Hood*, Cadfael willingly puts himself into a position where the murderer, Meurig, threatens him with a knife. Cadfael is trying to save Meurig's soul by getting him to repent for killing his father, to confess his sin, and to do penance.

In *One Corpse Too Many*, believing that justice requires an accounting, that God will preserve the innocent, and that the callous murderer of two men should not get away with it, Hugh Beringar challenges the taller, heavier, more experienced soldier, Adam Courcelle, to trial by combat to the death. Hugh's interest is also personal; one of the murdered men was his future wife's brother.

In *The Sanctuary Sparrow*, as one quarter of the men of Shrewsbury batter with murderous intent the poor, slight, young jongleur, Liliwin, seeking sanctuary in the abbey after being unjustly accused of theft and murder, Radulfus places his body between them and Liliwin. Picture this dramatic scene:

Abbot Radulfus, all the long, lean, muscular length of him, with his gaunt, authoritative lantern head blazing atop, sailed round the altar, smoky candle in hand, slashed the skirts of his habit like a whip across the stooping beast-faces of the foremost attackers, and with a long bony leg bestrode the fallen creature that clawed the fringes of the altar.

"Rabble, stand off! Blasphemers, quit this holy place and be ashamed. Back, before I blast your souls eternally!" (*Sparrow* 4)

Ellis Peters's final chronicle, *Brother Cadfael's Penance,* deserves to be treated separately, not only because it contains a culmination of many of her ideas on fatherhood, but also because it is unique in the series. Although the novel does not contain the customary romance with a happy ending, it is much more in the tradition of medieval romance than any of the previous Cadfael novels, featuring as it does a series of quests (Cadfael's for Olivier), medieval warfare (a detailed account of the siege of Philip FitzRobert's castle), disguises (Olivier's when he rescues Philip), spectacular deeds of bravery (Yves's climbing the huge vine to warn Philip of Empress Maud's intent to hang him), vengeance (Jovetta de Montors's killing of her son's murderer), and, above all, chivalrous, generous, honorable behavior on the part of many of the major characters. This honorable behavior is frequently connected to each character's role as a good father and underscores Peters's deep and abiding interest in the topic.

Seeing it as a higher obligation, Cadfael places his son Olivier de Bretagne's desperate need for help over his own soul's peace and happiness as a Benedictine brother. Cadfael breaks his solemn vows of obedience and stability when he ventures beyond the peace conference at Coventry to go to Olivier's aid, thereby risking expulsion from the Order. Like the Good Shepherd who would lay down his life for his sheep, Cadfael offers his life to Philip FitzRobert in exchange for Olivier's.

Cadfael protects, comforts, and secures the release from prison for the ardent, young Yves Hugonin with whom he had established a surrogate father relationship several years earlier in *The Virgin in the Ice.* Cadfael counsels Philip FitzRobert in his disillusionment and despair and helps to reconcile him with his estranged father, Earl Robert of Gloucester. Earl Robert mends the breach with his son and protects him from Empress Maud's sentence of death by hanging: "No man, not even the Empress, would touch what Earl Robert had blessed" (*Penance* 245).

Philip FitzRobert acts as a good father to his followers. To prevent them from being slaughtered by the forces of Empress Maud, Philip orders the surrender of his besieged castle. Realizing that there is no salvation in fighting for either King Stephen or Empress Maud and echoing the example of the seventeen-year-old Cadfael who went on the Crusade that established the Christian Kingdom of Jerusalem in the Holy Land, Philip FitzRobert takes the Cross and hopes to serve his Heavenly King by protecting Jerusalem from the Infidel.

Even a dark side of fatherhood is portrayed in *Brother Cadfael's Penance,* specifically in the tale of Lady Jovetta de Montors. She has a fierce love for her treacherously murdered son Geoffrey FitzClare and lives by a code of honor bred into the nobility. She exacts vengeance by killing her son's murderer and explains to Cadfael that she acted because the boy's father could not: "Richard was not living to do right by his son when he was most needed. It was left to me to take his place" (238).

At the end of this very satisfying novel, Abbot Radulfus, whose office it is to preserve all his flock, receives the prostrate but not penitent Cadfael (for he would make the same choice to go to his son's aid again) back into the monastery of Saint Peter and Saint Paul. In a beautifully healing moment of reconciliation, Radulfus utters the formal words of forgiveness and acceptance: " 'It is enough! Get up now and come with your brothers into the choir' " (*Penance* 255).

Ellis Peters proclaimed her most heartfelt beliefs about fatherhood when she wrote in reference to Earl Robert of Gloucester and his son Philip FitzRobert that the bond between father and son was "the most sacred and indissoluble tie that bound humankind. Nothing could break it" (*Penance* 153). Over and over again in her stories, Peters presented characters who reflect her belief in the strength of this bond of fatherhood, whether the fatherhood is biological, psychological, spiritual, or political. Surely it is no coincidence in many of Ellis Peters's novels that the strength of the loving bond between father and son or, by extension, between "parent" and "child" serves as a good predictor of the "child's" ability to relate happily to others as an adult, particularly in marriage. In expressing this truth about human nature, psychologists classify this ability to form mature, happy relationships as one of the benefits of secure attachment between "parent" and "child."

In her Cadfael Chronicles, Ellis Peters explored the various permutations of fatherhood with sensitivity and multidimensional understanding. Clearly the study of fathers in these fascinating mysteries offers readers a dense, colorful, many-faceted view of the rich life of medieval England.

Works Cited

Peters, Ellis. *Brother Cadfael's Penance*. New York: Mysterious, 1994.

——. *The Confession of Brother Haluin*. New York: Mysterious, 1988.

——. *The Leper of Saint Giles*. New York: Ballantine, 1981.

——. *A Morbid Taste for Bones*. New York: Ballantine, 1977.

——. *One Corpse Too Many*. New York: Ballantine, 1979.

——. *A Rare Benedictine*. New York: Mysterious, 1988.

——. *The Sanctuary Sparrow*. New York: Ballantine, 1983.

——. *The Summer of the Danes*. New York: Mysterious, 1991.

——. *The Virgin in the Ice*. New York: Ballantine, 1982.

Saints, Lepers, Beggars, and Pilgrims of Brother Cadfael

Anne K. Kaler

A thirteenth-century French miniature depicts two men approaching a leprosarium. One has a pocked face, carries a clapper and a begging bowl, has the broad-brimmed hat and surcote of the pilgrim, and is shod. He is the leper. To his right, however, is another smaller figure hobbling toward the sanctuary on crutches, hatless and shoeless with a single belted garment, holding his left leg up to show the bleeding wound on his shin. He is the beggar.[1]

The existence of such a miniature highlights the four stages of hospital care in the the early middle ages: the monk welcoming the unfortunates to the leprosarium; the institution itself named after a saint; the leper himself; and lastly the beggar or wanderer with the leg wound. When English novelist Edith Pargeter, writing as Ellis Peters, constructs the twelfth-century world of the Benedictine Brother Cadfael, she uses all four stages to characterize the extent of monastic care of the sick at Cadfael's abbey at Shrewsbury, especially in the *A Morbid Taste for Bones, The Leper of Saint Giles,* and *A Rare Benedictine.*[2]

By her choice of Saint Giles as her leperhouse, Peters honors a saint unfamiliar to modern audiences but the perfect and logical choice for Brother Cadfael whose godson, the son of Hugh and Aline Beringar, is named Giles. Furthermore, the author constructs her character of Guimar de Massard, the Lazarus of *The Leper of Saint Giles,* from those same elements which are associated with Saint Giles: the name Lazarus, leprosy, wandering, and the beggar with the leg wound.

The name of Saint Giles for her leper hospital is a logical choice for the author; the leperhouse founded in 1136, under the edict of the King and serviced by the Benedictine Abbey, gave rise to the town of Saint Giles. But why would a leperhouse be named after an obscure saint like Giles? Generally, names for hospitals were limited to a few saints whose names often signaled what disease was treated therein. A house for Magdalens specialized in prostitutes. Saint Roch, Saint Christopher, and Saint Sebastian warded off the arrows of plague. Saint Job or Saint Alexis covered indigents in general. But in England, a leper hospital was usually named after Saint Lazarus, Saint Bartholemew, or Saint Giles.

As the devotion to Christ's Passion increased with the iconography of graphic Spanish crucifixes and pictures, the image of the leprous beggar on crutches, barefoot and bleeding and bandaged head, coelesced into the figure of Saint Lazarus, a composite saint constructed from two figures from Christian Scriptures. In Christ's parable, Lazarus, the beggar who sat outside of Dives's gates where the dogs licked his wounds, received a higher place in heaven than the rich man (Luke 16:22-25). When the name degenerated until a *lazar* became the common term for any wanderer or afflicted person, it was assumed as the generic name for hospitals dedicated to the sheltering of lepers or wanderers. Unfortunately, by the time of Henry II, the word leper meant beggars or tramps; by 1525, in Spain, a *lazar* was a kitchen scullion who was later immortalized as a thief or street urchin in the picaro Lazarillo des Tormes.

The second figure is that of Lazarus of Bethany, whom Christ raised from the dead. Although there is no indication that he was a leper, his winding sheets suggested the white skin or scales of leprosy in the public mind. The motif of the wanderer also attached itself to the legends of this Lazarus, based on the tales of his sailing to Marseilles with his sisters to become the bishop of Aix-en-Provence. Saint Giles was also a wanderer who settled in Provence where his shrine was a waystation for pilgrims going to Compostela and the Holy Land.

Social need brings forth social action and the Crusades brought particular problems of returning soldiers who brought new diseases, which in turn brought forth new societies to help those afflicted. Although organizations of pious men such as the Knights Templar and the Order of Hospitallers took care of wounded or ill crusaders, the fear of leprosy was so great that a separate order, the Order of Saint Lazarus, was founded in Jerusalem early in the twelfth century for the care of crusaders afflicted with leprosy. What was unusual was that the soldier-monks were lepers themselves and it was not until centuries later that they admitted any non-leprous members. The Order was introduced into England during Stephen's reign with the founding of the leper hospital at Burton Saint Lazarus. The Order's seal has a bishop carrying a triune staff or a trident, probably representing the three-pieced wooden clappers of lepers.

Peters uses the name of Lazarus for her leper Guimar de Massard to identify him with the original Lazarus. Brother Mark, the Benedictine in charge of the leperhouse at Saint Giles, remarks that the man " 'says his name is Lazarus . . . a name he gave himself at a late christening . . . a second birth, lamentable though it may be. He was godfather at his own second baptism' " (14). At the end of the story, Guimar de Massard reinforces his connection with Lazarus, the man brought back from the dead, when he claims that he wants to remain dead because he is already " 'a dead man. Let my grave and my bones and my legend alone' " (215). The most direct reference occurs when Guimar uses a phrase reminiscent of both Christ's resurrection and that of the raising of Lazarus. In both cases a stone sealed the tomb but, while Christ ordered that the stone sealing Lazarus's tomb be rolled away (John 11:39), Guimar negates the order by his request of Cadfael: " 'Never seek to roll that stone away . . . I am content beneath it. Let me lie . . . for with the dead . . . all is very well' " (215-16). According to historical fact, Guimar de Massard could not have been helped by the Order of Saint Lazarus which was not established until 1142 in Jerusalem.

Despite this history, England more often used the wandering apostle of the east, Saint Bartholomew, as a patron for a hospital for contagious diseases. According to legend, the apostle Bartholemew who was flayed alive is pictured in iconography carrying his skin, hence his intercession in skin diseases such as leprosy. The Order of Saint Lazarus chose its master from among its members, but called him a "Bartholomew" (Barber 440). Although institutions such as Saint John's at Canterbury (founded by Archbishop Lanfranc between 1079-89), Saint Nicholas near

Harbledown, and Saint Leonard the Confessor's hospital in Northampton (founded in 1087) were leper hospitals, most leprosaria in England were dedicated to Saint Bartholomew, with fifty-five to Saint Leonard. The most famous Saint Bartholomew was founded in 1123 at Smithfield by the English courtier Rahere in gratitude for being cured of leprosy. Henry II founded another hospital by same name at Oxford in 1127-28 (Mitchie 63).

Most history books attribute the spread of leprosy with the returning crusaders but Mitchie sees the sudden endowment of leper hospitals as a guilt reflex by the nobility who "felt at risk from leprosy and therefore the leprosaria may have represented something of an insurance policy for the upper classes" (62) to relieve their consciences. Henry I endowed twenty-four leper-houses; Stephen endowed many monastic sites with the stipulation that their mission include care for the ill, which at that time meant of lepers. Since medical care in general was in the hands of the religious congregations who produced scientists and physicians, the leper hospital administered by a religious congregation is a given fact which Peters incorporates to construct her soldier-physician-monk.

Leprosy has long been a sacred malady. Saul Brody points out that one translation of the phrase "*quasi leprosum*" in Isaiah suggests that the Messiah might be one who "hath borne our infirmities and carried our sorrows: and we have thought him as it were a leper, and as one struck by God and afflicted" (53:4). Leprosy comes from a Greek work "lepra" meaning "scale" and Hebrew "*Tsar a'ath.*" The erroneous image of leprosy as being a white scale appears in Scriptures where King Uzziah of Judah is struck down as a "leper white as snow" as a punishment (2 Kings 5:27) and in Leviticus which describes leprosy as "a white color in the skin" (13:10).[3] Most societies isolate those afflicted with leprosy, both in life and in death; in some places, the church held an elaborate ceremony of "death" for the leper. Deprived of his family and wealth and status, driven outside the city, the leper who entered the living hell of the leperhouse could expect that his bones would be segregated also in a separate cemetery. It is these cemeteries which provide modern researchers with the skeletal remains to judge what kind and to what extent the person had leprosy.

While medical researchers are not certain of leprosy's origin, some propose that it mutated from the African disease of yaws. Researchers have ascertained that leprosy traveled from the Mediterranean coastal region into Britain in the fifth century A.D., spreading through skin-to-skin contact in small family groups and feudal communities where close living quarters and inadequate, shared clothing served to spread the disease. This same rural isolation slowed the general spread of the disease until the Conquest when the crowded and unsanitary towns encouraged the spread of airborne contagious diseases.[4] Leprosy peaked from the eleventh through the thirteenth century, then declined until it was almost gone by the sixteenth century, replaced by the more contagious tuberculosis (Manchester and Roberts 267).

However, judging from early Indian and Chinese records and the leprous remains of British leperosaria cemeteries, early medical professionals could distinguish between true leprosy and unrelated skin disorders. In her novel, Peters allows Cadfael to admire the skill of the Saracen doctors who treated Guimar and to explain the different symptoms of leprosy. She has him state with surety that "any man who broke out in nodes that turned to ulcers, or pallid, scaly eruptions of the skin, or running sores, was set down as a leper, though Cadfael had his suspicions that many such cases arose from uncleanliness, and many others from too little and too wretched food" (15-16). While the medieval belief was that rotten meat caused leprosy, Cadfael notes that proper diet and rest, the prescription of every leper-house, will effect most "cures." He recognizes that some skin infections, such as that suffered by Rhun, the leper woman's "scrofulous child with old drying sores in his thin fair hair" (6), can be cured by diet, care, or drugs such as the pellitory which Brother Mark has applied to the boy's head. Manchester and Roberts propose that "specific herbs (e.g., garlic, honeysuckle, nettle, scabious) [were used] for treating skin lesions associated with lepromatous leprosy" (270); pellitory or feverfew is derived from nettles. So effective is this care that Rhun is able to run errands in the town without notice once his sores are healed and once his "knock-kneed gait that stemmed from undernourishment" is abated (6). Although Cadfael knows that his "herbal remedies soothed and placated the mind as well as the skin" (1), because he knows that leprosy is easily spread to children, Cadfael tries to keep the boy away from the contagion of the lepers by placing him with the young lovers.

Peters has Cadfael further distinguish between the types of leprosy. The first type, lepromatous, is the most serious causing nodules and scaly patches on the skin until the skin becomes thickened and wrinkled and the face takes on a lionlike appearance. The thirteenth-century physician Gilbertus Angelicus noted this peculiarity in the signs of leprosy where the eyelashes and eyebrows are lost, the nose and cheeks turn into lumps, the face stiffens into a mask, the eyes become rigid, and the voice harsh (Rubin 156). Peters gives the destroyed face of the burntout leper to her Lazarus, a face "almost lipless . . . the nostrils eaten into great distended holes" (215) more in keeping with Cadfael's vision of leprosy as a "devouring demon [which] has died of its own greed" (14). Cadfael knows the difference between the kinds. The tubercularoid type has red, flat lesions on the skin which thickening produces anesthesia of the area. Peters's version of this occurs when Cadfael remembers his days as a crusader when men's skin would "whiten like ash, those whose skin powders away in gray patches . . . and who injure themselves, bleed, and are unaware of the injury" (15).

On the other hand, in creating her leper Guimar in *The Leper of Saint Giles*, Peters uses leprosy as a disfiguring but not a disabling disease. The disfiguring lesions of leprosy occur first in the skin, mucous membranes, and nerves but the destruction of the nerves and skin causes the disfigurement but not the loss of fingers and toes which are caused by secondary infections. When Cadfael refers to Lazarus as a "quenched fire" (215), Peters notes that Guimar bears the scars of burnt-out leprosy (or elephantiasis) in the thickened mask of scars which have immobilized his face and eaten off his fingers. Cadfael notes that Guimar's hand, which has "no ulcerous crust remaining; the seamed white flesh where the lost fingers had once been was dry and healed" (14), is the hand of a man whose leprosy has abated, though not without damage. Those missing fingers leave their distinctive mark which Cadfael recognizes on the throat of Picard. The detective also spots that young Joscelin is disguised as a leper when he sees his two complete hands instead of Guimar's malformed ones.

There were famous leperhouses which might have strengthened Peters's choice of Saint Giles. Queen Matilda nursed the lepers herself in the first London Leperhouse at Saint Giles. Of these twenty-four hospitals bearing the name of Saint Giles, twelve were leperhouses; of 750 hospitals, nearly two hundred were for lepers. Many of these were what Clay designates as "cottage hospitals" (xix), i.e., those small enough to be administered by a very small staff. Like other leperhouses, Cadfael's Saint Giles is meant to house only a small number—"twenty or thirty inmates" (5)—with great fluctuations of inhabitants due to weather, season, and choice. Thus the leperhouse was small enough to be ministered to by the relatively small Benedictine communities themselves but large enough to depend on the goodwill of the nearby townspeople.

The one saint who incorporated all the sympathetic features of beggar, wanderer, pilgrim, cripple, leper, and saint is Saint Giles. A sixth-century abbot of Arles also named Giles is often confused with Giles the Greater, who, according to Alban Butler's *Lives of the Saints,* was a seventh-century Athenian noble who fled Greece seeking solitude. He wandered France, settling in the desert near the Rhone, near the river Gard, and finally near the forest of Nimes where he lived on "wild herbs and roots and water" (3:401).[5] As his sanctity grew, others flocked to join him and holy legends about him sprang up. One states that he was wounded in the leg by the arrow of King Wamba while hunting a deer. Another is that he was nourished by the milk of that hind whom he defended and often fed. Another legend links Giles with the more famous third-century Martin of Tours, a Roman soldier who gave half his cloak to a beggar, only to have the beggar be Christ in disguise. When a sick beggar was miraculously cured by Giles throwing his cloak over him, he fled the adulation but quickly became known as a saint who could cure disease such as leprosy. Because leprosy cripples the limbs of its victims, Saint Giles was known as the saint of the cripples.

To strengthen this association, Peters makes much of Lazarus's limp, that "one-sided but steady and forceful gait of the old man" (12). Brother Mark's description is that of a resident doctor reporting to his superior instructor with a diagnosis on rounds: "he must be sadly maimed. You'll have noticed one foot is crippled? He has lost all toes on that one, but for the stump of the great toe, . . . I think the other foot may also be affected, but not so badly" (14). Although she describes Guimar as "a lame man, going upon one foot mangled by disease, he moved at surprising speed" (71) and is quite capable of hotfooting it off beyond the reach of the young people at the end of the tale. Thus, the predominant and recurring features of these legends—of beggars, of leprosy, of leg wounds, of a cloak—blended together to make Saint Giles a sympathetic saint for Peters to use as the name of a leper hospital operated by religious men who themselves have left the world behind.

Although the hospitals had stringent rules of conduct, most of them did not enforce strict segregation. Within the two hundred leper hospitals founded in England, isolation from society was the chief medicine and the salvation of the leper's soul was the goal of the religious administrators. Because leprosy bore the social stigma of sexual misconduct, it quickly became associated with syphilis and the physical revulsion of the disease grew into moral judgment of the person's past excesses. While this aspect does not enter Peters's story, she does make clear that the leperhouse is outside the town and away from the mainstream of society and, in doing so, the author again depends on Saint Giles's reputation as a hermit. He had, Cadfael notes, "deliberately chosen the desert and the solitary place for his habitation" (4) but he further remarks that Saint Giles had a choice while "these [lepers] had no choice but to remain apart [and] must also keep their distance even to do their begging in the countryside" (4). Often the leper hospital was outside the walls and shared the upkeep with the almshouse or infirmary for the sick and helpless near a hostel for passing pilgrims (Clay xix). One leper hospital founded in 1076 was referred to as a shelter outside the walls or "the house of pilgrims which is called the hospital [which included] *langwissying men greuyd with uariant sorys*" (Clay 3).

Although Chaucer's friar avoids the "sike lazars acquaintaunce" (Prologue l. 245) while his parson treats his people who have the "mesel," usual monastic care of the ill extended to both body and soul. The rule of Saint Benedict charged his followers to treat every guest as if they were Christ Himself and the bishops were enjoined to show mercy to "the poor, the stranger, and all in want" during their vows of consecration (Clay 2). Cadfael's Saint Giles never wants for volunteers to staff it; if a monk "attendant became the attended . . . there was never want of another volunteer to replace and nurse him" (5).

Peters uses all the symbols and conventions about Saint Giles in forming her leprosarium; it has a graveyard out in the back, it is staffed by members of a religious order whose pharmacist brings medicines. Her physical hospital includes a "modest enough church, nave and chancel and a north aisle, and a graveyard behind, with a carven stone cross set up in the middle of it" (4). This graveyard is of primary importance since by investigating cemeteries of leperhouses palaeopathologists can trace the progress and severity of the disease through the bones where most deformities occur in the hands, feet, skull, and lower limbs. Beauvais's miniature cited above shows the two forms of the outcast—the leper with his visible disease and the beggar or poor man with his wounded leg—which may be an early sign of syphilis. All are welcomed as inhabitants of the leperhouse.

Not all lepers were hospitalized just as Peters acknowledges that not all inhabitants of the leprosarium at Saint Giles were lepers. "Even when there were few lepers, for whose control and assistance the hospice existed, there were always some indigent and ailing souls in care there" (1). Those indigent and ailing souls were often people afflicted with other diseases while those remaining souls consisted of the beggar, the wanderer, and the pilgrim, worthy studies in themselves and certainly vital participants in Cadfael's world.

The character of the *vagus* or wanderer has a long history in English literature from Friar Tuck and other rogue monks to the picaro. Although the later mendicant orders of the Franciscans and the Dominicans were founded to bring the vernacular gospel to the people in the streets, early monks such as Benedictines and Carthusians were bound by a fourth vow of stability or loyalty to their specific institution, rather like the fealty owed by underlords to their overlords in the feudal system. Any breaking away from this vow seemed to disrupt stability, yet when Peters consistently writes about the wanderer, Cadfael is her prime example.

By capitalizing on a narrow period of history when the returning Crusaders—like Cadfael himself—were not unexpectedly classified as vagrants, Peters appeals to the restless and rootless flavor of modern times in her wanderers of the twelfth century. In *A Rare Benedictine*, the author has Cadfael as a landless man wondering about his future while wandering toward his home in Wales. His friend and ex-monk, Alard, describes his situation as "frivolous minds that must wander" (*Rare* 10).

Critics see "the First Crusade as spawning a new movement which both characterized and shaped Western Christendom for centuries [and which] was remembered as a symbol of loyalty and honour, a focus and inspiration for traditional secular qualities, not as a new way of salvation or a new form of war" or as Guibert of Nogent put it "as a new path of salvation which allowed laymen to earn redemption without changing their status and becoming monks" (Tyerman 552). Cadfael was in the First Crusade with Godfrey de Bouillon who took Antioch in 1098 and Jerusalem in 1099 where all inhabitants were slaughtered. His recall of this event allows him to recognize Guimar and to ascertain what he had suspected, that Guimar discovered his leprosy after his capture by the Saracens. There are actual precedents for such: historian Malcolm Barber cites the example of Robert of Zerdana who in 1119 was "still leading his troops in battle despite the fact that he was well known to be a leper even by his Muslim opponents, while King Baldwin IV led the Frankish army on several occasions" (449).

As a burnt-out case, Guimar is not contagious but his disfigurement which prevents him from rejoining society, especially that of the young lovers, also provides a handy disguise with its leper's cloak and veil. So, just as Peters models her leprosarium on Saint Giles, she combines the *vagus* or wandering man with the leper to create Lazarus, the quintessential wanderer who travels from leprosarium to hospital on an eternal journey rather like the Wandering Jew. It took Guimar eight years to cross Europe on "broken feet and with a clapper dish for baggage . . . with begging bowl and cloak and veil to make the endless pilgrimage to England" (214).

Peters's Guimar is cognizant of his role as a *vagus* and as a pilgrim: "'there's no relying on us wandering lepers, the pilgrim kind. We have minds incorrigibly *vagus*. The fit comes on us, and the wind blows us away like dust. Relics, we make our way where there are relics to console us'" (216). This last comment ties the themes together even more strongly since "Benedictine houses became the major repositories of relics and chief beneficiaries of the resultant pilgrimages and gifts . . . their shrines attracted as many pilgrims and penitents as any in Europe. Benedictines understood and fostered the sense of heavenly power associated with relics" (Van Engen 296). Of course, the first book of the chronicles *A Morbid Taste for Bones* centers on the acquiring of such relics.

Mixups often occur between lepers and *vagus*. The poor, as Christ said, will always be with us so that the religious impulse to serve the "pauperes Christi" is embodied in the Benedictine Rule. Because Benedict envisioned a voluntary lay community on the fringes of society rather than an organized monastery, the Benedictine rule "contained neither the word nor the concept of religious poverty as such" (Van Engen 285). Cadfael's monastery of Saint Peter and Saint Paul was founded in 1083 by Roger Earl of Montgomery, who died shortly after he became a monk in the house. By the time that Cadfael came to Shrewsbury, the Benedictine houses had begun to feel the drain of other monastic houses tapping into the financial pool. Land poor, the houses often resorted to disputes over land ownership to keep up with their good works and Peters capitalizes on these disputes in her series. But the work of serving God's poor directly extended into Cadfael's spiritual, pharmacist, and detective roles.

Beggars were not necessarily lepers. As the Beauvais miniature shows, the distinction between the two men arises from their different clothing. As a member of an elite group, the leper was given clothing and shoes, a cloak and a hat. The beggar, on the other hand, is in a ragged tunic, without cloak or hat, and without shoes which were expensive at that time. He also bears the significant leg wound which distinguishes him from the leper. Remember that the giving of the cloak to a beggar is the sign of a true saint. Saint Martin of Tours who divided his cloak with a beggar was just one of the many beggar saints; Saint Alexis, a fourth-century wanderer who left home on his wedding day, returned twenty years later as a beggar to live his life undetected under the stairs of his parents' home is another; Saint Roch, the patron of plague hospitals, had much the same story. Even John Lydgate called Saint Giles the "chief patryon . . . of pore foke" (Wilson 23).

Some lepers were also wanderers or pilgrims, whom Cadfael recognizes as "wanderers who made their way the length of the land from lazarhouse to lazarhouse, or settled for a while in some hermitage on the charity of a patron, before moving on to new solitude" (5). Margaret Lewis notes that Cadfael himself after a lifetime of wandering and settling in the abbey goes back to the "status of a vagus, and the wanderer, and he is grateful that his special skills allow him to move beyond the abbey walls to tend the sick" (98). However, the leperhouse at Saint Giles provides a natural outlet for Cadfael's restless energy because he can escape to it legitimately on errands to refill their pharmacy needs; he can advise the younger monks; and he can escape the confines of living with the same twenty men day after day.

Cadfael is the prototype of the wanderer in many ways: as a landless youth with itchy feet, to a Crusader foot-soldier at the battle of Acre, to a sea captain, to a stable monk, to a private detective or, as the modern parlance calls them, a "knight errant." His final wandering in *Brother Cadfael's Penance* is his most endearing journey, which anticipates the religious activities of the Mercedarians who offered themselves to the Moors in exchange for prisoners or slaves. When Cadfael offers to take his son's place to save the boy's life, he breaks his vow of religious stability to become an "outlaw" or "rogue" monk. He justifies his actions with the thought that his moral duty to his son preceded his vows to the abbey. In one sense, his journey is that of a hero on a pilgrimage back to the roots of his "sin" with Mariam and into the "hell" of Olivier's prison cell to rise again as he is accepted back into the stability of the abbey.

Although pilgrimages provided for the natural need to travel, not all pilgrims were on the road for religious causes. Fear of the unattached man or wandering rogue was a staple in medieval literature and society. Whereas the feudal society provided each person with a trade and a secure slot in life, the increase in travel and trade and warfare and Crusades which stirred the wanderlust in restless men—the picaro and the pilgrim, the journeyman and the peddler—contributed to the flow of society. Pestilence followed the same "song roads" of the minstrels and disease pursued the tradesman. Even Guimar admits that he is an "old leper who has preferred a night under the stars to the cover of a roof" (78). To accommodate the traveler, hospices were made available in monastic institutions, just as the Crusades spawned the orders of men dedicated to treating the victims of warfare. And the tales of the wandering saints are captured and used by the author in the legends of Saints Winifred and Beuno.

"Hagiography . . . includes both learned sophisticated Lives, akin to secular biography, and 'popular' Lives incorporating folk tales and fantasy" (Wilson 15). Peters combines the golden legend of saints' lives with the silver legend of popular lives in her use of the Welsh saints Beuno and Winifred. Written by an anchorite in the fourteenth century, a Welsh version of the life of Saint Beuno includes earlier material making him the northern counterpart of Saint David in South Wales. The historical Beuno, an abbot in North Wales who founded a monastery in Gwytherin, died in 660 A.D., and his bones were translated to Shrewsbury in the twelfth century. Like many Welsh saints, Beuno's connection with a holy well offered water to cure sick children who were left all night in his tomb; his cult survived the Reformation and lasted up to 1770. Like the Celtic *peregrini* who travelled to more and more deserted places seeking solitude, Beuno's cult spread so much that churches named after him seemed to spawn other daughter churches named after his "relatives" or "pupils" or "fellow religious."[6]

This is what happened to Saint Winifred who is accounted as Beuno's niece in several tales. What connects the stories and what may be a very good reason Peters chooses this uncle-and-niece combination is the linking device of the cloak. Every year Saint Winifred sent a cloak to Beuno by placing it on the river which magically conveyed the cloak to him no matter where he was.

Peters's version of the cloak appears in the "crumpled, empty garments" of the dead Brother Columbanus's clothes carefully arranged to establish his being taken into heaven by Saint Winifred when all the time Cadfael has arranged Columbanus's body to replace that of the saint in the reliquary (*Bones* 211). The same theme appears in Peters's use of Butler's tale of the virgin's attacker Caradoc (Cradog to Peters) who also is "melted away" when Saint Beuno condemns him (Butler 55).

The efficacy of holy wells and waters is treated both in legends and in treatment of leprosy. Butler claims that mosses around Saint Winifred's well which cures "stubborn and malignant diseases such as leprosy" sprang from the healing fountain where her severed head landed and the stones remained tinged with red blood.[7] Sir Roger Bodenham was cured of leprosy in 1606 (Butler 268 fn.); the mother of Henry VIII built a chapel on the spot; and the cult survived the Reformation to the point where Samuel Johnson noted that people still bathed in her well. After the Dissolution, the only relic of hers was taken to Holywell where she had allegedly lived most of her life as a nun.

The cult of Saint Winifred outdistanced even Saint Beuno's fame as a miracle worker with its "ancient, widespread, and persistent character of her cult" (Farmer 441). As often happens in hagiography, the story raises the girl's struggle to save her virginity to the level of martyrdom and miraculous recovery. When Caradoc, the son of the prince, tried to seduce Saint Winifred with a promise of marriage and failed, he beheaded her outside the church or chapel where, at the intercession of her uncle Saint Beuno, she was raised from the dead. A manuscript on her life appears in the Cottonian library manuscript, Claudius A., written by a monk at Basingwerk soon after the Conquest. A second life by Robert, prior of Shrewsbury, gives the account of the translation of her bones in 1138 where her relics were enshrined in the abbey church. This, of course, is the source of Peters's first Cadfael novel, *A Morbid Taste for Bones,* and provides a stable theme for all the Chronicles of Brother Cadfael.

At a time when pious pilgrimage slowly fell into picaresque wandering, Cadfael reverses the process to settle down into a Benedictine monastery. Just as Saint Giles was associated with leprosy, a lame leg, a beggar, a wandering spirit, and a desert hermetical experience, so also is Guimar or Lazarus a leprous, lamed, begging, wanderer seeking solitude and forgiveness after retribution and revenge. If Cadfael occasionally wanders off in pursuit of the truth, he is forgiven by his faithful readers who rejoice in his dogged search for truth in the human soul and the Divine Mind. His transgressions can be forgiven as easily as he is forgiven by his abbot in the last book *Brother Cadfael's Penance* for his many kindnesses to the saint, the leper, the pilgrim, the wanderer, and the beggar.

Notes

1. Vincent of Beauvais, *Miroir Historicl*. Bibliotheque de l'Arsenal, Paris, MS 5080, The Bettman Archive in David Reisman, *The Story of Medicine in the Middle Ages* (New York: Hoeber/Macmillan, 1936) plate 9.

2. All references are to *The Leper of Saint Giles* unless otherwise noted.

3. Also, "Naaman the Syrian was cleansed off the leprosy in these water [Jordan], and his flesh came again in the flesh of a little child" (2 Kings 5).

4. William McNeill in *Plagues and People* stresses that the Black Death which decimated the population may have been a blessing because it increased the chances for people to have more clothing and food: "even the poor were able to cover their bodies more completely than before, and in so doing Europeans may very well have interrupted the older patterns of skin to skin dissemination used by Hansen's disease and by yaws. If so, the emptying out of Europe's leprosaria becomes readily understandable" (158). He feels that leprosy was often mistaken for yaws which is spread by human contact and produces open wounds similar to leprosy.

5. In subsequent years a Benedictine monastery grew up and the town named Saint Giles became the center of activity against the Albigensian heresy and the site of a major pilgrimage shrine. Although he is not a martyr, Giles is mentioned by Bede and Ado (Butler 401).

6. Bowen attributes the development of the cults of Saint Beuno and Saint Winifred to the ease of travel on the Roman roads.

7. The legend of Saint Winifred's being beheaded is probably the misinterpretation of iconography. When the saints hold their heads in

their hands or when they have red circles around their necks, it indicates martyrdom but not necessarily beheading. In fact, the most common way of killing a young girl was not to behead her—that was saved for the sturdier men who might have the physical strength to object. Rather the executioner used jugulation or the rupturing of the jugular vein. Because jugulation was not as dramatic as beheading, the story tellers took liberties to heighten the drama.

Works Cited

Barber, Malcolm. "The Order of Saint Lazarus and the Crusades." *The Catholic Historical Review* 53 (July 1994): 439-56.

Bowen, E. G. *The Settlements of the Celtic Saints in Wales*. Cardiff: U of Wales P, 1956.

Brody, Saul Nathaniel. *The Disease of the Soul: Leprosy in Medieval Literature*. Ithaca: Cornell UP, 1974.

Butler, Alban. *The Lives of the Fathers, Martyrs, and Other Principal Saints*. 4 vols. Baltimore: Murphy, 1860.

Clay, Rotha Mary. *The Medieval Hospitals of England*. London: Frank Cass, 1909, 1966.

Farmer, David Hugh. *Oxford Dictionary of Saints*. 2nd ed. New York: Oxford UP, 1987.

Hole, Christina. *English Saints and Sanctuaries*. London: Batsford, 1954.

——. *Saints in Folklore*. New York: Barrows, 1965.

Lewis, Margaret B. *Edith Pargeter: Ellis Peters*. Bridgend Midglamorgan, Wales: Seren, 1994.

Manchester, Keith, and Charlotte Roberts. "The Palaeopathology of Leprosy in Britain: A Review." *World Archaeology* 21 (Oct. 1989): 265-72.

McNeill, William. *Plagues and People*. Garden City, NY: Anchor, 1976.

Mitchie, Colin. "Saint Bartholomew's of Oxford." *History Today* 41 (Dec. 1991): 62-63.

Peters, Ellis [Edith Pargeter]. *Brother Cadfael's Penance*. New York: Mysterious, 1994.

——. *The Leper of Saint Giles*. 1981. New York: Quality, 1990.

——. *A Morbid Taste for Bones*. New York: Fawcett Crest, 1978.

——. *A Rare Benedictine*. New York: Mysterious, 1989.

Rubin, Stanley. *Medieval English Medicine*. New York: Barnes and Noble, 1974.

Tyerman, C. J. "Were There Any Crusades in the Twelfth Century?" *The English Historical Review* 110.437 (June 1995): 553.

Van Engen, John. "The Crisis of Cenobitism Reconsidered: Benedictine Monasticism in the Years 1050-1150." *Speculum* 61 (Apr. 1986): 269-304.

Wilson, Stephen, ed. *Saints and Their Cults: Studies in Religious Sociology, Folklore, and History*. Cambridge: Cambridge UP, 1983.

The Ministries of Brother Cadfael

Soldier, Sailor, Cleric, Celt:
The Philosophy of Brother Cadfael

Kayla McKinney Wiggins

Devoted fans of the Cadfael series by Welsh/English author Ellis Peters (Edith Pargeter) would probably agree that a major component in the power of the series is the character of Cadfael himself. Former soldier, sailor, and man-of-the-world, Cadfael comes to rest at age forty in the monastery of Saint Peter and Saint Paul at Shrewsbury, content to be a part of a brotherhood and renounce the world, but seldom sorry to see the world intrude on his solitude and call him forth again to action. Much of the commentary generated by the Cadfael series has centered on the philosophy/theology/ideology of Cadfael. Mary K. Boyd, in "Brother Cadfael: Renaissance Man of the Twentieth Century," argues that Cadfael is a product of his times, a man of the twelfth-century Renaissance. William David Spencer, in *Mysterium and Mystery: The Clerical Crime Novel*, argues that Cadfael creates his own theology—at times "hyper-Calvinistic," at times "all merciful universalism"—to suit the situation and his concern that "whatever insight can be gained by contemplation is obviously negligible compared to that gained by experience" (67-68). Peters herself, in an interview with Ed Christian and Blake Lindsey, agrees with her interviewers that Cadfael is a "Situation Ethicist," basing his actions in any given situation on "the correct thing to do" rather than "on a strict moral code" (18). And, of course, everyone agrees that Cadfael's position as a Catholic monk influences his world view. I would argue, however, that Cadfael's ideology grows directly out of his Welsh heritage, out of a Celtic sense of society and cosmology.

Any study of the ancient Celts is likely to generate conflict, paradox, and confusion. Researchers agree about little in regard to these ancestors of Western culture. The Celts were either barbaric, warring tribes marginally civilized by the Greeks and Romans, or highly advanced artisans and philosophers who contributed their own humanistic ideology to the philosophies of Greece and Rome. They were either peaceably assimilated into the complex stratum of cultures that converged to create English society between the fourth and the eleventh century, or were virtually eradicated by the brutality of their conquerors. What scholars and historians do seem to agree on concerning the Celts is that they were a tribal people, skilled artists and craftsmen, warriors, herdsmen, and farmers, who moved from the Rhineland across much of Europe during the first millennium B. C. E. The various tribes that made up the Celtic world shared a common world view, lifestyle, and language that they passed on to their more modern descendants—the Irish, Scots, Manx, Welsh, Cornish, and Bretons.

Ellis Peters, in the introduction to *A Rare Benedictine,* explains her choice for the name of her protagonist, saying that she was looking for something unique. "His name was chosen as being so rare that I can find it only once in Welsh history, and even in that instance it disappears almost as soon as it is bestowed in baptism" (2). The historical Cadfael in question, Saint Cradog, though christened Cadfael, was known always as Cradog. However, there is another Cadfael in Celtic history. According to Celtic historian Peter Berresford Ellis, there was a seventh-century king of Gwynedd named Cadfael ap Cynfedw. According to the Welsh triads, this Cadfael was one of three kings whose lineage was "sprung from the villeins"; the name means "battle chief" or "battle seizer" (Ellis, *Celt* 115), not an unfitting choice for a commoner and former crusader. However unique his name, Cadfael is definitely set apart from his monastic brothers. In the first place, he is very much a man of the world, having settled to the monastic life only after forty years of wide-ranging experience that included, as he explains to Brother Mark in *The Summer of the Danes,* working for a wool merchant, fighting in the Crusades, and captaining a ship. He has a wide knowledge of plants, herbs, and medicines, both in their beneficial and their harmful uses, as well as of the ills that beset humankind spiritually, emotionally, and physically. He has seen more of pain and death than most of his brothers can imagine, but he holds always a benevolent tolerance for human failings, not out of a sheltered innocence but out of a considered knowledge of the diversity of the human condition. He is tolerant of the young, of women, of love and sexuality, remembering with pleasure his time in the world and regretting none of it, a position that would shock his more sheltered fellows, many of whom have been cloistered from childhood. What most sets Cadfael apart, however, is his Welshness, his Celtic sense of society and cosmology.

As Margaret Lewis points out in *Edith Pargeter: Ellis Peters,* borderlands "are lands of tension, where cultures clash and tensions linger," but they are also areas that "signify diversity" (9, 10). This is certainly true of the Welsh/English world of Shrewsbury. Of the twenty novels in the Cadfael series, four of them: *A Morbid Taste for Bones, Monk's-Hood, Dead Man's Ransom,* and *The Summer of the Danes* are set partly in Wales and deal with things Welsh. *A Morbid Taste for Bones,* the first novel in the series, was originally intended to be a single novel based around the history of Shrewsbury Abbey and Saint Winifred. The novel is a fictionalized account of a historical event, the acquisition by the Abbey of Saint Peter and Saint Paul of the bones of the Welsh Saint Winifred. Peters has said that, given the nature of her intent in this novel to chronicle the trip to and from Wales, together with her own fascinating subtext of murder and revenge, it was necessary to create a Welsh protagonist who was nonetheless a Benedictine monk and a man of wide-ranging experience (Lewis 83-84, 89-90). Thus, Brother Cadfael was born, and a series was unexpectedly launched.

As we find out in *A Morbid Taste for Bones,* Cadfael comes of "antique Welsh stock" (9), and he is at home in the ancient Celtic sense of society that saw no paradox in wedding an outspoken self-determination with a close sense of community. Many of the customs of the ancient Celts still exist in Cadfael's Welsh world, virtually unchanged through the centuries. He knows them, and applauds their operation in the person-centered Welsh (Celtic) social structure.

The ancient Celts were a tribal people, living in a close-knit clan system, with each individual having a voice. Cadfael is comfortably aware of his own individual voice, and not hesitant to make others aware of it, yet he is also one of a community. As a young man, he left Wales because he was not content with "a slip of land" of his own (Peters, *Summer* 62) but wanted to see the world, leaving one community only to find others, the community of the crusaders and eventually the community of the brothers in Shrewsbury. Despite his sense of belonging to a community of brethren and to a rule of order and religious service, Cadfael is not hesitant to abjure community when necessary, nor to break the rule if expediency demands. This attitude extends even to breaking faith with his Abbot in the last book of the series, *Brother Cadfael's Penance,* when a stronger tie of kinship—that with his son—takes him away from the brotherhood and toward his own journey of self-discovery.

The ancient Celts were an agricultural people who lived on independent homesteads, based their wealth in cattle, and practiced an economic system based on barter. The lifestyles of the Welsh in *A Morbid Taste for Bones* illustrate the fact that not much has changed over the centuries in the Celtic world. The people still live on independent farms, closely bound by bonds of kinship; they have little use for money as indicated by their disdain for bribery; and they rear cattle as their major livelihood, with even a run-away English youth finding his place as a caller to lead the teams as they plow. Hospitality was an important social force in the ancient Celtic world, as it remains in Cadfael's Wales. Even though they resent the ploy to take from them "their holiest girl," the gentle priest of Gwytherin and the people of the area extend themselves to offer comfort and hospitality to the brothers from Shrewsbury because the rules of hospitality were a sacred trust and "Guests were sacrosanct" (*Morbid* 39, 35).

As sacred as the duty of hospitality was the duty of vengeance, with provision made in the ancient laws for a blood price or *glanas* to be paid for certain crimes, including homicide, to prevent the destructiveness of a blood feud. Each person had a price, and each could go surety for another, offering his life in payment if the other should forfeit honor or violate a sworn oath. This system becomes a major force in a later Welsh-based novel, *Dead Man's Ransom,* as a young man, Eliud, finds himself pledging his life for the forfeit honor of his foster brother Elis.

Eliud rides into battle with archers at his back, and around his neck the noose that will hang him if the oath remains unfulfilled. Fosterage, a system whereby young men and women of noble birth were reared by aristocrats other than their parents, was widely practiced by the ancient Celts. This custom created a bond between foster siblings that was stronger even than the bond between natural siblings. As a Welshman, Cadfael understands the depth of this bond: "'Kin by fostering can be as close as brothers by blood, I know'" (*Ransom* 30). He suffers with the foster brothers in *Dead Man's Ransom* when their bond is put to the ultimate test. Each young man heroically offers his life for the other, Eliud in battle, flinging himself between his foster brother and a Welsh arrow, and Elis to the law in payment for his foster brother's crime of murder.

Equally heroic and supremely Celtic is the moment in the novel when Elis stands in defiance of his Welsh brethren, protecting a convent of holy women from the warring ravages of a vengeful band of Welsh raiders. He holds them off with nothing more than a homemade weapon and the power of his Welsh voice. Riding through the forest toward the scene of battle, the captive Eliud and his English escort hear the sound of a Welsh voice raised in defiance.

The challenge had meant nothing to Herbard. It meant everything to Eliud. For the words were Welsh, and the voice was the voice of Elis, high and imperious, honed sharp by desperation, bidding his fellow-countrymen: "Stand and turn! For shame on your fathers, to come whetting your teeth on holy women! Go back where you came from and find a fight that does you some credit!" (*Ransom* 161)

As Eliud flings himself away from his captors and toward where his foster brother is standing off an angry war-band with nothing more than the force of his bardic tongue, Elis's voice rings on in scathing defiance:

Cowards of Powys, afraid to come north and meddle with men! They'll sing you in Gwynedd for this noble venture, how you jumped a brook and showed yourself heroes against women older than your mothers, and a world more honest. Even your drabs of dams will disown you for this. You and your mongrel pedigrees shall be known for ever by the songs we'll make. (*Ransom* 162-63)

This speech is in true druidic tradition, right out of the ancient Celtic world. The druids had the power of scorn in their tongues, cursing their victims with shame. So powerful was the *glam dicin*—"a form of lampoon with the potency of a spell which at one extreme could be used to drive out rats and at the other to disable, even kill, a human victim"—that even mighty heroes like Cu Chulainn lay down their arms in fear of the curse (Rutherford, *Celtic Mythology* 35).

The Celts were fine artists and craftsmen who valued above all the artistry of the spoken word. The bards kept the histories, the genealogies, and the legends. They were honored above almost all others, and every great lord kept his own poet to make the music and sing the songs. Again, this tradition figures in *A Morbid Taste for Bones* when the resident poet sings the funeral songs for Rhisiart, the champion cut down because of his defense of Saint Winifred against the English monks who have come to remove her to England. This tradition also runs strong in the blood of Brother Cadfael who finds his voice unleashed when he is called upon to defend the Welsh Saint Winifred from the intended desecration by the English monks, translating "with the large declamation of the bards" (*Morbid* 39).

However, the Celts were also a warring people and the blood-lust, a rampant joy of battle, was a vital part of their culture. Cadfael, despite his position as a man of peace, as a Benedictine brother, and a representative of God on Earth, shares this thrill at battle. Many times throughout the twenty-novel series he is a witness or participant at a scene of violence, and while he holds his hand and does no harm to any, his Celtic blood rises in response to the thrust of battle. In pursuit of the murderer in *A Morbid Taste for Bones,* he rolls "like a thunderbolt down the narrow path through the graveyard" with the Welsh-woman, Sioned, her blood also up, in his wake (222). In *Monk's-Hood* his blood rises when he is accused of improper thoughts toward a woman and he longs to ring the scrawny neck of his accuser, the falsely pious brother Jerome. In *The Pilgrim of Hate* he goes bellowing through the woods to stop a murder "shamelessly exulting" (132). And in *The Summer of the Danes* he rushes toward, not away from, the sounds of battle, wondering even as he runs at his own response and provocation.

Despite the violence of the time, truth and justice were so valued in the Celtic world that at every Welsh coronation, bards recited verses reminding the new king of "the necessity of reigning justly to prevent famine or plague from falling on his people" (Rutherford, *Celtic Lore* 106). As Peter Berresford Ellis points out in *Celt and Saxon,* the Welsh legal system was a humanistic one, respecting the rights of individuals and stressing just compensation for loss rather than a continuance of vengeance. Perhaps such a concept seems paradoxical in a world that also stressed the importance of vengeance for the loss of a loved one, but the same culture that conceived the blood feud also conceived the honor-price, a valuation set on every life that could substitute honor, surety, and justice for death. The goal in a harsh world was to preserve life, not to perpetuate the killing. This concept operates throughout the Cadfael series, but it receives a pseudo-official status in the Welsh novels.

In *A Morbid Taste for Bones,* Cadfael pits himself against the official vengeance of the Catholic Church by covering up a death that was self-defense in Welsh eyes, but would have been treated as murder by the English church. He is aided in his careful maneuverings by the entire population of the Welsh community that houses the bones of Saint Winifred. In *Dead Man's Ransom* he must turn a blind eye to the removal of Eliud back to Wales to protect him from certain conviction and execution as a murderer. Had Eliud stayed in the jurisdiction of English law, Hugh Beringar, the sheriff of Shrewsbury and Cadfael's confidant and friend, would certainly have had to, however reluctantly, execute him. In *The Pilgrim of Hate,* a novel not set in Wales but dealing heavily with things Welsh as it concerns the miraculous operations of Saint Winifred, a young English nobleman elects compassion over vengeance against the murderer of his lord and foster-father, and Cadfael and Hugh again look the other way as the murderer flees into Wales.

Cadfael himself expresses this attitude of mercy in *Monk's-Hood,* a novel set partially in Wales and centering on the action of the Welsh legal system. When the son of Richildis, Cadfael's former beloved, is accused of murdering his stepfather, Cadfael steps in to protect the young man and solve the murder, a solution that only becomes possible when Cadfael realizes that the land of the dead man is in Welsh territory and subject to Welsh law. When he attends the Welsh court where evidence is the witness of neighbors, Cadfael finds what he has expected, the illegitimate son of the dead man claiming inheritance because in the Welsh system a son was a son, no matter on what side of the sheets he was born. In the Celtic, and the Cadfael, system of justice, murder, while it may keep a young man from inheriting the land he claims, does not necessarily demand a life for a life. When Cadfael denounces and proves this illegitimate son as the murderer of his father, the young man in question comes seeking his own form of justice, with a knife at Cadfael's throat, only to recant and beg forgiveness when Cadfael stands bravely facing death. Begged by the murderer to pass judgment, Cadfael offers not the death sentence but a life of penance. In the eyes of the kinship, this young man has lost everything—birthright, land, name, and kinship—yet Cadfael gives him back his life. He says

"I rule that you shall live out your life—and may it be long!—and pay back all your debts by having regard to those who inhabit this world with you. The tale of your good may yet outweigh a thousand times the tale of your evil." (*Monks-Hood* 206)

For Cadfael, each life taken is a life lost, a potential good gone out of the world. Better far, as in the old Celtic way, that payment be made, and some new good added to the debt of the world.

In regard to women, the ancient Celtic world was far removed from Cadfael's England. The medieval world greatly restricted the scope of women. Laws and social customs limited their ability to own property, take legal action, and be independent human beings. Even in Cadfael's Wales the place of women is limited, though it is less limited than that of women in England. The women of Gwytherin cannot attend the meeting to decide the fate of their patron saint even though they share her gender. Sioned, the young noblewoman in love with an outlander in the novel, cannot marry according to her choice, but must accede to her father's wish. However, most of the women in the twenty novels of the series, whether Welsh or English, show an independence of spirit that does credit to the ancient Celtic world where women were equals in marriage and accorded protection in the eyes of the law, where they could own property, lead tribes, become warriors, and even lead in battle. In regard to his attitudes toward women, Cadfael is more a Celt than either a Welshman or a Benedictine. Despite a certain sexism (in *Monk's-Hood* he thinks of Richildis as "a sweet woman, but dangerous, like all her innocent kind" [110], and in *A Morbid Taste for Bones* he reflects on his past sexual relationships with women concluding that they had been "pleasurable to both parties, and no harm to either" [7], a conclusion that might be questioned by the women involved), Cadfael certainly does not think of women as the downfall of society as do most of his monastic brothers. Women, seen through Cadfael's eyes, are in most cases the strongest characters in the novels, independent, self-determining, mature, and beautiful in spirit as well as body. He is their champion and protector, as he is the champion and protector of the young and the dispossessed.

Obviously, Celtic society, like their legal system, was humanistic and people-centered. So is Cadfael's view of society. He cares little for law and officialdom; he cares much for the elderly, the young, women, and the dispossessed. His sense of justice is mitigated by a strong sense of compassion, tempered like fine steel by a worldly assessment of human triumphs and failures. In short, Cadfael values people over rules or organizations, as did his ancestors the Celts.

Celtic cosmology and Celtic Christianity, which grew in part from it, are equally humanistic. In an interview in *Clues* magazine, Ellis Peters said, when asked if she saw any Protestant leaning in Cadfael, " 'No, I think what does survive in him is his inclination to the Celtic Christianity'" (21). As the Welsh novels of the Cadfael series make clear, Celtic Christianity was grounded in the individual's relationship with God; it was centered more in the hermitage than the monastery, with clerics who were participating members of the tribal society and, more often than not, married. According to Nora Chadwick, the eminent Celtic scholar, the Christianity of the Celts stressed a "serene inner life" (219). Cadfael does indeed draw on this heritage, often going alone in supplication to God and even withholding confession of some of his more suspect actions until such time as his beloved former assistant Mark can be ordained. In his supplications and his occasional self-doubts, he is drawn particularly to Saint Winifred, the Welsh saint he took from the soil in Gwytherin and returned to that same soil. He treasures being out in God's world, working in his garden, going on rambles, and adjusting the shortcomings of his fellow sojourners in this life, as much as participating in the communal offices of the church. In his solitary supplications to God and the saint, in his love for the soil and the Earth, Brother Cadfael practices a cosmology and theology akin to that of his ancient ancestors.

According to the classical writers, the ancient Celts believed in the immortality of the soul, that after this life there would be another much the same. Modern authors have interpreted this belief in various ways. Peter Berresford Ellis comments that "the Celts were one of the first cultures to evolve a sophisticated doctrine of the immortality of the soul. The druids taught that death is only a changing of place and that life goes on with all its forms and goods in the Otherworld" (*Dictionary* 14). While Stuart Piggot acknowledges (and perhaps puts undue stress on) the druidic role as priest, he also discounts the Celts as a barbaric culture with merely the trappings of civilization, and doubts the advanced state of philosophy ascribed to a druid by Cicero because the druid probably could not speak Latin (40, 104). T. D. Kendrick claims that the Celtic belief in an afterlife was nothing more than a primitive philosophy because it did not include a system of punishment for the wicked and reward for the good in that other life (143). If this is the standard that separates Christianity and ancient Celtic beliefs, Cadfael in his benevolent humanism would seem to be closer to the latter than the former. While he is quite aware that God will sort all, he is also quite content to leave that sorting to God, and to trust that God will be as forgiving and understanding in regard to the failings of frail human beings as he is.

In addition to their concept of the immortality of the soul, the Celtic people felt a strong affinity to the Earth, believing in an organic totality, a unity between this life and the next, between nature and humanity. They saw the land as a living, sacred entity and recognized no separation between religion and living, seeing all life as a religious expression (Stewart 23). Cadfael exhibits this sense of cosmology, celebrating all activity in the open, whether it is working with his beloved herbs or harvesting crops. He abhors a sickly white tonsure and celebrates the natural world. In much the same way, he and the novels celebrate the seasons, moving inexorably forward, closely tied to that ancient Celtic world that measured its cattle-rearing, agricultural existence by the four major seasonal celebrations of Imbloc, Beltaine, Lugnasad, and Samain. Ellis Peters agrees that "season plays a big part. In fact, the books proceed season by season, very much. I like that continuity" (Christian 25).

The ancient Celts saw a close connection between this world and the Otherworld, seeing the ancient sidh, the barrows of the ancestors, as sacred places, entrances to the Otherworld of the gods and the supernatural. Springs and wells were also entrances to the Otherworld and, in the transfer from the pagan to the Christian world, these sacred sites took on Christian overtones, becoming the sacred locations of saints. The holy well of Saint Winifred in *A Morbid Taste for Bones* could be such a site. Certainly the story of the martyrdom of Winifred—with the decapitation, the melting of her tormentor, and the restoration of her life—bears druidic overtones. Druids had the power to cause such destruction to those who displeased them, and decapitation forms a major motif in the myths and legends of the Celtic people. In the ancient Irish story of Bran the Blessed, Bran's severed head becomes a companion for his former warriors, advising and guiding them for years. Decapitation also served as a form of intimidation to enemies and a celebration of victory in battle.

When Cadfael takes Saint Winifred's bones from the Welsh soil, he feels a reverence for them that goes beyond his sense of her as a saint and his identity as a brother of the same faith. She is a Welshwoman, one of his kin, one of his blood. He thinks of her as young and her bones tell him that she was slender and beautiful. His reverence for her is a reverence born of his respect for her humanity, not of any superstitious awe at miraculous stories of life restored or of bodies that don't decompose. Later, when he returns her to that earth, bedding her with the body of her Welsh champion, he is as sure of her desire to be served in such a way as he is of her ability to guide the living to the just ends so served. And still later, in *The Pilgrim of Hate,* when he goes to her in supplication seeking a sign of her approval of his actions, he is comforted by the miracles she does for him, not one but three: the healing of Rhun, the return of Olivier, and the resolution of the conflict without the cost of another life.

The ancient Celts believed in a cycle of life, feeling that death was simply a progression in that cycle. Theirs was an "exuberant" philosophy "which had no regrets for life nor fear of death: death was simply a passing of place, and life continued in the Otherworld" (Ellis, *Celt and Saxon* 52). When the Celts accepted Christianity, this philosophy was reinforced in the concept of a Christian "Land of Eternal Youth" (Ellis, *Celt and Saxon* 52). Cadfael has such an acceptance of death. When in *Monk's-Hood* he stands with a murderer's knife at his throat, he does not flinch, and when the murderer whispers in his ear to ask incredulously if he isn't afraid of death, he says, " 'I've brushed elbows with him before. We respect each other. In any case there's no evading him for ever . . . Here am I as you willed it. Now take what you want of me' " (202-03). Admittedly, Cadfael does not believe this young man is a true murderer, but that in no way negates the strength of his philosophy. He knows that death will come, this night or another, by this hand or some other agency. He will not evade it, and he will not fear it. Death is a part of life. From the moment we are born, we are dying. God will sort all, and we need not fear the Otherworld anymore than we fear this one.

Ellis Peters once said, " 'I'm definitely not a feminist. I'm a humanist' " (Christian 17). Like his creator, in his acceptance of life, death, the cosmos, and other fallible human beings, Brother Cadfael—crusader, sailor, cleric, and Celt—is last and best a humanist. He respects and admires the best in human beings and forgives the worst. And he knows that the majority of us will fall somewhere in between.

Works Cited

Boyd, Mary K. "Brother Cadfael: Renaissance Man of the Twentieth Century." *Clues* 9 (1988): 39-48.

Chadwick, Nora. *The Celts.* London: Penguin, 1971.

Christian, Ed, and Blake Lindsey. "Detecting Brother Cadfael: An Interview with Ellis Peters, 17 August 1991." *Clues* 14.2 (1993): 1-29.

Ellis, Peter Berresford. *Celt and Saxon: The Struggle for Britain AD 410-937.* London: Constable, 1988.

——. *Dictionary of Celtic Mythology.* Oxford UP, 1992.

Kendrick, T. D. *The Druids.* 1927. London: Senate, 1994.

Lewis, Margaret. *Edith Pargeter: Ellis Peters.* Border Lines Series. Bridgend Mid Glamorgan: Seren, 1994.

Peters, Ellis [Edith Pargeter]. *Brother Cadfael's Penance.* New York: Mysterious P, 1994.

——. *Dead Man's Ransom.* New York: Morrow, 1984.

——. *Monk's-Hood.* New York: Fawcett Crest, 1980.

——. *A Morbid Taste for Bones.* New York: Fawcett Crest, 1977.

——. *The Pilgrim of Hate.* New York: Morrow, 1984.

——. *A Rare Benedictine.* New York: Mysterious P, 1988.

——. *The Summer of the Danes.* New York: Mysterious P, 1991.

Piggott, Stuart. *The Druids.* 1968. London: Thames and Hudson, 1975.

Powell, T. G. E. *The Celts.* 1958. London: Thames and Hudson, 1980.

Rutherford, Ward. *Celtic Lore.* London: Thorsons, 1993.

——. *Celtic Mythology.* New York: Sterling, 1990.

Spencer, William David. *Mysterium and Mystery: The Clerical Crime Novel.* Ann Arbor: UMI Research, 1989.

Stewart, R. J. *Celtic Gods, Celtic Goddesses.* London: Blandford, 1994.

Stephen or Maud:
Brother Cadfael's Discernment

Marcia J. Songer

In her Brother Cadfael mysteries, Ellis Peters carefully recreates the Middle Ages. The novels, or chronicles as Peters calls them, are peopled with monks, lords and ladies, and returned Crusaders. Setting is such an important component that, in many of the novels, Peters provides maps of the environs of Shrewsbury where events are taking place. To establish time, she not only gives specific dates but also incorporates elements of the power struggle between King Stephen and Empress Matilda.

As grandchildren of William the Conqueror, both Stephen and Matilda had viable claims to the throne. Matilda, called Maud by the English, was the daughter of Henry I, son of William. When his only legitimate son drowned, Henry tried to ensure the succession by twice getting his barons to swear oaths of allegiance to his daughter. After Maud was widowed from the Holy Roman Emperor Henry V, her father married her to Geoffrey of Anjou. It was a political move meant to nullify the threat of Anjou, a traditional enemy, to Henry I's Norman territories.

However, when Henry died in 1135, Maud was with Geoffrey in Anjou, and it was Stephen, son of William's daughter Adela, who beat her to London and claimed the crown. Because many of the barons were unhappy with the prospect of a female ruler, who would undoubtedly be ruled by her husband, they abandoned their oaths and supported Stephen. Others remained faithful to Maud. The resultant civil war raged with varying intensity until 1153.

Ellis Peters uses the civil war as an effective backdrop to the Cadfael series. Outwardly, Brother Cadfael takes no side in the war. His experience in the world and his native intuition make him a perceptive judge of people, and he aids those on both sides of the conflict according to individual merit rather than political cause. After years of fighting in the Crusades, his principal desire is for peace. However, despite Cadfael's attempt to remain neutral, the reader detects a preference that peace come with Stephen on the throne. How discerning is Cadfael's judgment in leaning toward Stephen rather than Maud? Ellis Peters's research into the period becomes evident in her portrayal of this inclination. Were Cadfael a real monk choosing between the contenders as history portrays them, he would make the same choice.

In Peters's novels, Cadfael develops his preference gradually. In fact, there is no one to prefer in the first novel, *A Morbid Taste for Bones*. No specific date is given, and no mention is made of the struggle between Stephen and Maud. It is only with the second novel, *One Corpse Too Many*, that Peters decides to weave historical events into the plots. Then she sets the date as August 1138, and the chronicles move forward from that time. The civil war is a central focus of the second chronicle. Supporters of the empress hold the castle at Shrewsbury while Stephen and his forces have the town under siege. The reader is introduced to Stephen almost immediately. He is far from a perfect ruler. The conflict between his "natural indolence" (*Corpse* 170) and his desire for quick results, between his compassion and his need for vengeance, often befuddles his adherents. Cadfael observes, "Energy and lethargy, generosity and spite, shrewd action and incomprehensible inaction, would always alternate and startle in King Stephen. But somewhere within that tall, comely, simple-minded person there was a grain of nobility hidden" (*Corpse* 59).

Hugh Beringar is also introduced in the second chronicle when he offers his support to Stephen. By the end of the novel, Stephen has captured Shrewsbury and made Hugh deputy sheriff of the shire. Despite a budding friendship with the likable young Hugh, at this point Cadfael feels no allegiance for either of the contending sovereigns and can maintain his earlier declaration: "[M]y monarch is neither Stephen nor Maud, and in all my life and all my fighting I've fought for only one king" (*Corpse* 33).

The events of the ensuing novels follow the events of the civil war. By the third chronicle, Pope Innocent has acknowledged Stephen's claim to the throne while Maud is pressing her case in Rome. She does not, however, do anything in England to encourage her supporters until the fifth chronicle when she arrives from the continent "with her half-brother Robert, earl of Gloucester, and a hundred and forty knights, and through the misplaced generosity of the king, or the dishonest advice of some of his false friends, [is] allowed to reach Bristol" (*Leper* 4).

As Maud and Stephen grapple for power, Cadfael still remains aloof from partisanship. In the sixth chronicle, he consoles a young girl concerned about her uncle's ties to the empress: "I have told you, I take no side here, and Hugh Beringar would not expect me to go always his way in every particular. He does his work and I do mine" (*Virgin* 98). Hugh's work consists not only of helping defend the castle of Shrewsbury but also of leading the feudal levies of soldiers furnished by King Stephen. After returning from battle at Lincoln, Hugh explains why Stephen abandoned his hilltop advantage there: "Why, with that mad chivalry of his, for which God knows I love him though I curse him, he orders his array down from the height into the plain, to meet his enemy on equal terms" (*Dead* 8). Little wonder that Cadfael can later think, "Surely there never had been such a king as Stephen for conjuring defeat out of victory" (*Confession* 7).

Frustrated as he is with Stephen's chivalry, Hugh remains in awe of his talents on the field of battle. Despite them, Stephen is captured and imprisoned at Bristol while his wife gathers forces to attempt his release. Hugh observes that although one can find no better fighter than Stephen, his queen is a better general: "She holds to her purpose, where he tires and goes off after another quarry" (*Pilgrim* 4).

By the tenth chronicle, after four years of order maintained by the king's men, the inhabitants of Shropshire have grown used "to thinking of the king's cause as their own" (*Pilgrim* 15). Perhaps Cadfael is also accustomed to thinking of the king's cause as the cause of the shire. Surely his by now staunch friendship with Hugh and the fact that he is godfather to Hugh's son give him reason to feel comfortable on Stephen's side.

Despite trying to maintain neutrality, in this chronicle he expresses some doubt. While giving Hugh advice, he exclaims, "God forgive me, why am I advising you, who have no prince in this world!" However, he admits to himself he is "none too sure about the truth of that, having had brief, remembered dealings with Stephen himself, and liked the man, even at his ill-advised worst" (*Pilgrim* 26).

As events march on, the advantage continues to shift. With Stephen in chains, the empress is in London expecting to be crowned when she is forced to leave and take refuge at Winchester. Peters writes:

A good many coats had been changed in haste after that reversal, not least that of Stephen's brother and Maud's cousin, Henry of Blois, Bishop of Winchester and papal legate, who had delicately hedged his wager and come round to the winning side, only to find that he would have done well to drag his feet a little longer. For the fool woman, with the table spread for her at Westminster and the crown all but touching her hair, had seen fit to conduct herself in so arrogant and overbearing a manner towards the citizens of London that they had risen in fury to drive her out in ignominious flight, and let King Stephen's valiant queen into the city in her place. (*Excellent* 4)

Maud's arrogance and lack of discretion are mentioned several times even by those on her side. The liege man of one of her supporters admits, " 'I knew . . . she was not wise—the Empress Maud. I knew she could not forget grudges, no matter how sorely she needed to close her eyes to them. I have seen her strip a man's dignity from him when he came submissive, offering support' " (*Pilgrim* 196).

Maud takes refuge in Winchester, which is soon besieged by Stephen's queen. As Maud's capture seems imminent, Cadfael hopes for an exchange, even if that means starting the contest all over again. As it turns out, it is not Maud but Robert of Gloucester who is taken prisoner at Winchester, yet the effect is almost the same. An exchange is finally carried out and Stephen is freed.

In the twelfth chronicle, Hugh Beringar is invited by Stephen to his Christmas feast and returns confirmed in the office of sheriff, a position he has held unratified since the death of his predecessor. He comments on the king's remembrance of how Hugh first became deputy and adds, "I fancy that's a rare touch in kings, part of the reason why we cling to Stephen even when he maddens us" (*Raven* 83). That common touch, the generosity, the thoughtfulness seem to offset Stephen's lack of tenacity and judgment, not only in Hugh's eyes but in Cadfael's as well.

In the late chronicles, the empress is under siege at Oxford but escapes. She sends to her husband in Normandy for help, but he is busy conquering Stephen's Norman territories. Instead of sending troops, he sends their son, the future Henry II. In the fifteenth chronicle, Peters writes:

In the five years that King Stephen and his cousin, the Empress Maud, had fought for the throne of England, fortune had swung between them like a pendulum many times, presenting the cup of victory to each in erratic turn, only to snatch it away again untasted, and offer it tantalizingly to the other contender. (*Confession* 2)

Ellis Peters is faithful to history in many elements she includes in her books. Although Eudo Blount, a landowner in *The Potter's Field*, goes to help fight at the seige of Oxford, Hugh states that his " 'only due was an esquire, armed and mounted, for forty days' " (7). John Beeler explains that it was probably during Stephen's reign that the select *fyrd* was changed from sixty to forty days (101), and he stresses the importance of such levies in conducting " 'the siege warfare characteristic of the period' " (100). He points out that the " 'infantry levies were usually commanded by the sheriffs, or other representatives of the crown' " (102-03) just as Hugh commands the troops from his shire. If Peters is accurate in those details, it is not surprising that she is also accurate in portraying character.

John Appleby suggests that the conflicting qualities in Stephen's character can be traced to his parents. From his father " 'Stephen inherited a charming and happy disposition, an ability to please and get on well with others, and the daring and bravery that inspired the elder Stephen in the brighter moments of his career. His inheritance from his mother showed only occasionally in ill-inspired fits of sternness' " (18).

From the earliest accounts, Stephen's complex personality comes through. The monk writing the *Anglo-Saxon Chronicle* credits him with being "a mild man, and soft, and good" (207) even while complaining that those qualities and his inability to execute justice enabled the rich to get away with unprecedented anarchy and pillage. He details some of the worst deeds committed during Stephen's reign of nineteen winters, a time when "they said openly, that Christ slept, and his saints" (208).

Because Maud's half-brother Robert was the patron of William of Malmesbury, one does not expect that historian to give an unbiased view. William points out that Stephen was among those who swore oaths to support the empress, oaths which he obviously ignored. Still he admits that Stephen was "a man of activity, but imprudent: strenuous in war; of great mind in attempting works of difficulty; mild and compassionate to his enemies, and affable to all." He adds that he was kind "as far as promise went; but sure to disappoint in its truth and execution" (491). He also concedes that before he came to the throne Stephen, "from his complacency of manners, and readiness to joke, and sit, and regale, even with low people, had gained so much on their affections, as is hardly to be conceived" (493).

Henry of Huntingdon, Archdeacon of Lincoln, gives "listening to perfidious counsel" (272) as the reason Stephen granted Matilda a safe conduct to Bristol when she first arrived in England. Ordericus Vitalis says of that action, "[P]rudent men regret that he was regardless of his own welfare and the kingdom's security. It was in his power at this time to have easily stifled a flame which threatened great mischief" (212). Ordericus was a Norman monk whose father founded the abbey of St. Peter and St. Paul at Shrewsbury, the very abbey where Cadfael tends the herb garden. Ordericus writes that Stephen "was condescending and courteous to those who were good and quiet, and, if his treacherous nobles had allowed it, he would have put an end to their nefarious enterprises, and been a generous protector and benevolent friend of the country" (218).

The author of the *Gesta Stephani*, thought to be Robert of Lewes, Bishop of Bath and a protege of Bishop Henry, explains that Stephen was "the dearest of all his nephews to King Henry," not just because of family ties but because of "conspicuous virtues. He was in fact a thing acknowledged to be very uncommon among the rich of the present day, rich and at the same time unassuming, generous, and courteous." The writer goes on to say that in war and in siege he was "bold and brave, judicious and patient" (5). The fact that he adds *judicious* and *patient* might make the reader call into question all the other characteristics, were those characteristics not confirmed by other authors. The writer states that at the beginning of his reign, Stephen "showed himself good-natured and agreeable to all" (23).

Three of Stephen's contemporary historians rail against his handling of the church, its property, and its freedom, but all three who complained were clerics. It takes a current historian to put their objections into perspective. Z. N. Brooke explains that the papacy took advantage of the dissension during Stephen's rule to assert itself. Henry I had controlled ecclesiastical appointments and maintained much of the barrier William I had established between England and Rome (165-67). Because Stephen owed his crown to papal sanction, he granted the freedoms the church asked for. The bishops became papal, not royal, officials, many of them appointed by Bishop Henry. Then, when Stephen moved against those within the church who were politically dangerous to him, the church complained that he was infringing on its freedom (187). Brooke points out that "Matilda was much more formidable and dangerous to freedom" (188), a fact which contributed to Bishop Henry's abandonment of her and return to the support of Stephen, albeit with reservations.

Austin Poole analyzes Stephen's suitability for the throne. In addition to having spent years at the court of Henry I and having been knighted by Henry himself, in both England and Normandy,

he was well known and deservedly popular; for, in striking contrast to his two Norman predecessors, he was a man of an attractive personality. He was not, like them, hard and avaricious; he was a brave, generous, simple-minded man who in any other walk of life would probably have succeeded admirably. . . . His faults were lack of statesmanship and of decision and firmness. He had not the ability or the strength of character necessary to deal with the very difficult situation that confronted him. (132)

Although historians heap both blame and praise on Stephen, they seem to have nothing favorable at all to say about Matilda. Poole explains that because of her marriage to the Holy Roman Emperor "she had been brought up in Germany where alone she was appreciated and even regarded with affection. . . . [What the English people] had learnt of her they did not like, for she was a disagreeable woman, haughty, tactless, and grasping" (131). Nicholas of Mont Saint-Jacques, her contemporary, writes of her, "The woman is of the race of tyrants" (qtd. in Z. N. Brooke 207).

The *Gesta Stephani* author reveals that as soon as Stephen was captured, Matilda "at once put on an extremely arrogant demeanour" (119) and

on being raised with such splendour and distinction to this pre-eminent position, began to be arbitrary, or rather headstrong, in all that she did. Some former adherents of the king, who had agreed to submit themselves and what was theirs to her, she received ungraciously and at times with unconcealed annoyance, others she drove from her presence in fury after insulting and threatening them. (121)

Henry of Huntingdon was no partisan of Stephen, but he says that Matilda "was elated with insufferable pride at the success of her adherents in the uncertain vicissitudes of war, so that she alienated from her the hearts of most men" (280).

All historians, contemporary and current, agree that the reign of Stephen was a troubled time, but current ones provide some new assessments of the period. Christopher Brooke declares, "In England Stephen's reign was remembered, with some exaggeration, as nineteen years of chaos, anarchy, and suffering. In fact, the anarchy was intermittent and often local, and the later years of the reign were less severe than those which followed the Empress's invasion in 1139" (166-67). Richardson and Sayles describe the disorder encountered by Henry II when he succeeded Stephen, but they contend, "To this disorder the Empress and, more particularly, her son had been principal contributors to the very end of Stephen's reign. To say this is not to impute blame: it is to state fact" (264).

The Cadfael series reveals Ellis Peters's thorough grounding in twelfth-century history. It is evident that Peters has studied early historians for the detail of places, events, and customs. She has looked at both medieval and contemporary evaluations of personalities. In Cadfael, she has created a character who bases his judgment on real traits of the two contenders for the throne. Like him, a real Brother Cadfael would have prayed for Stephen's final victory.

Works Cited

Anglo-Saxon Chronicle. Trans. James Ingram. 1912. New York: Dutton, 1934.

Appleby, John T. *The Troubled Reign of King Stephen.* New York: Barnes, 1970.

Beeler, John. W*arfare in Feudal Europe 730-1200.* Ithaca: Cornell UP, 1971.

Brooke, Christopher. *From Alfred to Henry III 871-1272.* Vol. 2 of *A History of England.* Ed. Christopher Brooke and Denis Mack Smith. Edinburgh: Nelson, 1961.

Brooke, Z. N. *The English Church and the Papacy from the Conquest to the Reign of John.* 1952. Cambridge: Cambridge UP, 1968.

Gesta Stephani. Ed. and trans. K. R. Potter. Oxford: Oxford UP, 1976.

Henry of Huntingdon. *Chronicle.* Trans. and ed. Thomas Forester. 1853. New York: AMS, 1968.

Ordericus Vitalis. *The Ecclesiastical History of England and Normandy.* Vol. 4. Trans. Thomas Forester. 1856. New York: AMS, 1968.

Peters, Ellis. *The Confession of Brother Haluin.* New York: Mysterious, 1988.

——. *Dead Man's Ransom.* 1984. New York: Ballantine, 1986.

——. *An Excellent Mystery.* 1985. New York: Ballantine, 1987

——. *The Leper of Saint Giles.* 1981. New York: Ballantine, 1985.

——. *One Corpse Too Many.* 1979. New York: Ballantine, 1985.

——. *The Pilgrim of Hate.* 1984. New York: Ballantine, 1987.

——. *The Potter's Field.* New York: Mysterious, 1990.

——. *The Raven in the Foregate.* 1986. New York: Ballantine, 1988.

——. *The Virgin in the Ice.* 1982. New York: Ballantine, 1984.

Poole, Austin Lane. *From Domesday Book to Magna Carta 1087-1216*. 2nd ed. 1955. Oxford: Oxford UP, 1975.

Richardson, H. G., and G. O. Sayles. *The Governance of Mediaeval England from the Conquest to the Magna Carta*. 1963. Edinburgh: Edinburgh UP, 1964.

William of Malmesbury. *Chronicle of the Kings of England*. Ed. J. C. Giles. 1847. New York: AMS, 1968.

Cadfael and the Borders

Margaret Lewis

Over nine hundred years ago the island of Britain was invaded for the last time. William of Normandy succeeded in capturing the English throne in 1066 and with ruthless efficiency he installed Norman authority in all parts of the kingdom. But even he had to accept that there were limits to the extent of his administration. To the west and to the north the Welsh and the Scots stubbornly resisted this well-organized but alien power.

The Norman ascendancy responded with a series of castles defending its authority in the Marches or borders of Wales and Scotland. By the end of the eleventh century a line of stone-built, turretted castles, often built on the edge of an escarpment for ultimate defensive power, stretched from Chester to Montgomery in the west and along the shifting Scottish border in the north: "the debatable lands." The castles reinforced earlier lines of demarcation, such as Offa's Dyke, a ditch boundary which King Offa of Mercia ran down the border with Wales in the eighth century and which can still be followed today. The mountains of Wales were obvious barriers to invading armies and only starvation could eventually drive out highly mobile bands of warriors. In the north, Hadrian's Wall, built between 122 and 127 AD, remained the centre of a fluctuating border that was not to be settled until the union of the crowns of England and Scotland in 1603. The Wall remains as a reminder of the vulnerability of even the firmest borders, yet even now as the tourist stands there, looking first north and then to the south, the real differences between the two kingdoms become very clear. To the north stretches open moorland with heather and sheep; to the south, well-kept fields and boundaries. For centuries, such border areas would never be at peace.

Shrewsbury Castle was one of the earliest Norman border outpost, built by Roger de Montgomery in 1083. It was in a fine defensive position, rearing proudly high up on a peninsula above the River Severn and accessible only by two bridges, to the west and to the east. Shrewsbury, therefore, was a frontier town and remained so throughout Brother Cadfael's sojourn as a Benedictine brother in the Abbey of Saint Peter and Saint Paul.

In considering the significance of the Borders in the *Cadfael Chronicles*, it is useful to remind ourselves of Edith Pargeter's particular affection for the Welsh. Although she herself was born and lived all her life in Shropshire, she placed a special value on the heritage she received from her Welsh grandmother, Emma Ellis. The name Ellis was passed on to two of her grandchildren; Edith's brother was called Edmund Ellis Pargeter and Edith chose it for her most famous pseudonym, Ellis Peters.

For someone who responded above all to deeds of bravery and individual courage, the resistance of the Celts to the imposition of outside rule was inspiring material for fiction. *The Heaven Tree* trilogy, which was set in the dangerous no-man's-land of the Marches, the buffer zone between England and Wales, and the *Brothers of Gwynedd* quartet, which deals with the Welsh struggle to create an independent kingdom in the thirteenth century, are outstanding examples of historical fiction. Edith regarded them as being among her finest work. Meticulously researched, these novels engage the reader in a world of complex relationships between aggressive Welsh princes and powerful English barons. To the reader at the end of the twentieth century there is endless fascination in the sights, sounds, and smells of these evocative novels. The feel of a heavy oak door pulling shut in draughty castles, the welcome sight to a weary traveller of a hall brightly lit by braziers and flares, the sense of danger in the chink of a bridle in the depths of a dark wood—all this revealing detail of a past world is effortlessly woven into a gripping narrative. There are many competent writers of historical fiction who do their research and present a worthy piece of work. But very few can achieve what Ellis Peters has done, to bring the reader into an acceptance of her created world, no matter how distanced it is in historical time.

By the time Edith Pargeter came to write *A Morbid Taste for Bones* in 1977 she was steeped in the history of Wales and the Borders. *The Brothers of Gwynedd* and *The Heaven Tree* had crystallized a lifetime of interest and many hours of patient research in libraries and archives. Not that she found this other than a pleasure. We are considering here a person who purchased the two-volume *History of Shrewsbury* for £5 when she was just a teenager, when £5 must have been very hard to come by; someone for whom the past was a kind of electric force arising out of everyday life. But not only did she respond to the politics and historical events of the time, she was able to grasp the hidden lives of history. As the historian Professor Helen Cam wisely observes:

Historical fiction is not only a respectable literary form: it is a standing reminder of the fact that history is about human beings. However much the student is concerned with statistics or ideologies or "trends" or institutions, the fact remains that every statistical item represents some outcome of human activity, every ideology issues from a human brain, every "trend" is a pattern imposed by human thinkers on human doings, and every institution is composed of and operated by human individuals. (6)

The town of Shrewsbury and the Abbey of Saint Peter and Saint Paul are well populated through Peters's imagination, but her fictional world is firmly based in historical fact.

The presence of the nearby border was a defining force in the early history of Shrewsbury Abbey and this influenced both the character of Brother Cadfael and the plots that were created around him. No doubt if Peters had placed her horticultural hero in Winchester or Saint Albans there would have been enough political and social tensions to keep him busy and to provide ample material for her novels. But a setting on the Welsh borders, with a hero who was Welsh but under oath to a Norman foundation, that surely opened up a promising storehouse of interesting material. Not only that, the narrow streets of Shrewsbury and the ruined castles and abbeys of Shropshire were imprinted deep into her everyday experience as well as her imagination. The old merchants' houses and "shuts" or alleyways of Shrewsbury did not need to be researched, nor did the riverbanks of the river Severn as it meandered easily south of the town. She had walked these riverbanks since childhood and had explored the many winding roads that climbed exhilaratingly up to the hills of Wales to the west.

Cadfael ap Meilyr ap Dafydd of Trefriw comes as an outsider to Shrewsbury Abbey and he remains so, from beyond the border; an outsider on the inside. The tension between him and the aristocratic Norman, Prior Robert, is an essential part of every novel, and the shared knowledge of Cadfael's great deception grows with every book. Hugh Beringar, who takes over from Gilbert Prestcote as Sheriff, of necessity supports the Norman structure of government, but he is sufficiently astute to look the other way if he feels that Cadfael is on the right track, but on the wrong side of the law. Cadfael is devoted to his calling as herbalist and healer, but he is nevertheless always delighted to have the prospect before him of a ride outside the city with a good horse under him, preferably bound for the rolling hills of Wales.

As the chronicles unfold, the author takes her hero and the mysteries he is investigating northwest across Offa's Dyke into Wales, to Rhydycroesau and Glen Ceriog, and to Bangor and Aber. *Dead Man's Ransom* is set up here, and part of *Monk's-Hood*. Most of *The Summer of the Danes* takes place in the brilliant light of the coastal area around the Lavan sands, beneath the towering head of Mount Snowdon. Moving south to Bromfield and the Clee Hills, Peters give us the unforgettable landscapes of *The Virgin in the Ice*, and pictures a silent Shropshire, blanketed in heavy snow, its streams and lakes frozen, providing the grave for a young and beautiful victim of violent crime. *The Hermit of Eyton Forest* takes Brother Cadfael to Buildwas Abbey and Haughmond, and *The Potter's Field* to the banks of the Severn near Shrewsbury. The commercial life of the prosperous city of Shrewsbury itself is at the heart of many novels, particularly with detailed descriptions of crafts and trades which were connected to the wool trade with Wales.

But again, as with the creation of Midshire in her contemporary crime novels, there is more to the border landscape than gently flowing rivers and blue remembered hills—there are the people. In 1140 the Welsh, the Normans, and the English were still very different nationalities. Peters's books are constantly alert to Welsh individualism and cultural identity, which in historical terms came to triumphant fruition with the Treaty of Montgomery in 1267 and the recognition of Wales as an independent principality.

Throughout the Cadfael novels the Welsh are clearly defined as being very different to the English, and in many cases much wiser, too. Their language, their song, their Celtic faith, their system of law are all distinctive and many novels hinge on these differences. In *Monk's-Hood,* for instance, the ancient Welsh court convicts the criminal for a murder committed in England, but there is much sympathy for someone driven to murder by intense love of the land on which he was raised. Inexplicable carelessness on the part of Brother Cadfael leads to his escape westwards, followed by prayers for his redemption. This is not the only novel where swift flight from Shrewsbury across the border into Wales is the only solution to a complex problem.

So the border offers escape, and it also offers contrast. England is seen as becoming settled, with stone buildings and established towns. William's famous Domesday book of 1085-86 noted all the property under Norman rule and established a firm basis for ownership and responsibility. An indignant monk at Peterborough wrote in the Anglo-Saxon Chronicle that "So narrowly did he cause the survey to be made, that there was not one single hide nor rood of land, nor—it is shameful to tell but he thought it no shame to do—was there an ox, cow, or swine that was not set down in the writ" (Smith 38). The Welsh, on the other hand, lived lightly on the land in wooden houses scattered along river banks or in the woods, or, like the warrior princes, moved swiftly from camp to camp in the folded border hills. Many distinctive aspects of Welsh society are revealed as Peters develops the *Cadfael Chronicles*, such as the limited use of coinage in economic life.

The border is of pressing interest in the first novel, *A Morbid Taste for Bones*, because the need for Shrewsbury Abbey to have a saint worthy of veneration drives Prior Robert into Wales to lay claim to a Celtic saint, Winifred:

He had been scouring the borderlands for a spare saint now for a year or more, looking hopefully towards Wales, where it was well known that holy men and women had been common as mushrooms in autumn in the past, and as little regarded. (14-15)

The community of Gwytherin, where the saint is buried, clearly shows how different the rule of law is in Wales from Norman law across the border. Prior Robert assumes that his authority and a ruling from on high is suffcent to enforce obedience, and he is surprised at the local priest's insistence on consulting the entire community. When the Welsh congregation challenges Prior Robert's claim to the saint, it is seen as "a Welsh voice that cried battle," and the aristocratic Prior recoils "into marble rage under Welsh siege" (*Bones* 51).

Norman princes who dismissed the Welsh as savage barbarians understood very little of the subtleties of Welsh law. Professor John Davies describes it in his *History of Wales:*

The Law is among the most splendid creations of the culture of the Welsh. For centuries it was a powerful symbol of their unity and identity, as powerful indeed as their language, for—like the literary language—the Law was the same in its essence in all parts of Wales. The Law of Hywel was not a body of law created de novo; it was the systematization of the legal customs which had developed in Wales over the centuries. The Law of Wales, therefore, was folk law rather than state law and its emphasis was upon ensuring reconciliation between kinship groups rather than upon keeping order through punishment. (88)

Welsh Law, then, was much more democratic in its structures, as was the Church in Wales, providing fundamental differences in the ways of regulating society. It was also very accommodating to fugitives from English justice. As Cadfael remarks about a fugitive in *The Sanctuary Sparrow,* "once well into Wales he can thumb his nose at the sheriff of Shropshire" (234). The route into Wales was not difficult (only about twelve miles as the crow flies) and the prospects were good, as we learn in this novel:

Owain Gwynedd, the formidable lord of much of Wales, withheld his hand courteously from interfering in England's fratricidal war, and very cannily looked after his own interests, host to whoever fled his enemy, friend to whoever brought him useful information. The borders of Shrewsbury he did not threaten. He had far more to gain by holding aloof. But his own firm border he maintained with every severity. It was a good night, and a good time of night, for fugitives to ride to the west, if their tribal references were good. (*Sparrow* 235)

Engelard, the ox-caller in *A Morbid Taste for Bones* is also a fugitive, having escaped across the border because of his enthusiastic deer-poaching on the estates of Earl Ranulf of Chester. (It is an interesting detail that in Wales the oxen are encouraged to pull the plough by calling them from in front, rather than goading them from behind. This says much about the Welsh character.) Engelard is a cunning hunter with the short bow and will inherit his father's manor in England in due course. Meanwhile he flourishes in Wales, safe from Norman justice which would probably lead to having his hands chopped off for this crime.

Not only is Norman justice harsh, it also countenances slavery. In *The Holy Thief*, Daalny, a singer in the entourage of the Provençal Troubadour Rémy of Pertuis, escapes her destiny as a slave by heading west into Wales in the company of another musician, Tutilo, both knowing how valued their music will be: "'Better go naked into Wales, and take your voice and your psaltery with you, and they'll know a gift from God, and take you in'" (243), advises Daalny knowingly. Tutilo disappears into the night, and Daalny, after clearing his name, joins him to follow the old Roman road south of the town that goes straight into Wales.

This background of resistance to authority and uneasiness at obeying orders from outside powers is very much part of the character of Brother Cadfael. He pushes against the borders of his calling as well as against the borders of his shire. In many novels his inability to make his vow of obedience to the Rule accord with what he wants to do, and feels that he must do according to his innate sense of justice, forms an important part of the plot. The most extreme case of disobedience occurs in the final novel, *Brother Cadfael's Penance*, when he does not return to the Abbey as instructed and sets off instead to search for his missing son, Olivier. He is well aware of the consequences:

It was like the breaking of a tight constriction which had bound his life safely within him, though at the cost of pain; and the abrupt removal of the restriction was mingled relief and terror, both intense. The ease of being loose in the world came first, and only gradually did the horror of the release enter and overwhelm him. For he was recreant, he had exiled himself, knowing well what he was doing. (*Penance* 97)

During his penitential journey back to Shrewsbury, through floods and storms, he wrestles with the problem of obedience and sin, sin as defined by the Ordinances of the church, but not, he regrets, according to his own morality: "If the sin is one which, with all our will to do right, we cannot regret, can it truly be a sin?" (*Penance* 267). Cadfael is fortunate that Abbot Radulfus has some understanding of Celtic subtlety as the prodigal is brought back into the fold.

The physical border of dyke and mountain is, of course, buttressed by the essential component of language. No country can maintain its independence once language is lost, and the Welsh today maintain a keen defence of their Celtic tongue. As soon as the border has been crossed, the present-day traveller is confronted with bilingual signs, and as the roads lead further to the west, English becomes less and less prominent. Welsh language schools, churches, and a Welsh language television station help to keep Welsh as the first language for many people.

Brother Cadfael's fluent Welsh provides a useful plot device in many novels. Sometimes he is sent as an interpreter with groups of English clerics, as in *A Morbid Taste for Bones* or *The Summer of the Danes*, although one can question whether the translations are always strictly impartial. Cadfael's bardic blood can run away with him at times. But any good intelligence officer is at home in the language of the other side, and Cadfael falls easily into the company of Welsh villagers who are able to help him unravel many puzzling events as the ale passes round.

The Welsh often pretend to know less English than they do, a trick that is used skilfully by the cunning merchant Rhodri in

Saint Peter's Fair. Cadfael is asked to be his interpreter, but neither is taken in. As they say farewell after an eventful fair, where Shrewsbury has taken on the role of a kind of Medieval Berlin with spies and intelligencers from all parts, Cadfael understands very well that Rhodri has been in Shrewsbury to collect information for Owain Gwynedd about the political situation along the border, and lets him know it:

"Now I come to think," mused Cadfael, "it would be excellent cover for Owain's intelligencers to ask the help of an interpreter in these parts, and be seen to need him. Tongues wag more freely before the deaf man."

"A good thought,"approved Rhodri. "Someone should suggest it to Owain." (*Saint Peter's* 173)

Throughout the twenty novels, two major strands of history create tension against which the plots develop, the civil war in England between the forces of King Stephen and the Empress Maud, and the uneasy relationships between the Welsh princes. Generally speaking the Welsh stay on their own side of the border, but occasionally young blood sees the challenge of the border as too much to resist. In *Dead Man's Ransom* both conflicts come together. The original sheriff of Shropshire, Gilbert Prestcote is injured and taken captive while fighting for the King in the Fens of Lincolnshire. He is carried back to Wales by mercenaries and is held to ransom. Cadfael negotiates an exchange of prisoners with Owain, but complications arise when an undisciplined band of warriors from another tribe plan a raid on a vulnerable cell of nuns at Godric's Ford, very near the actual border with Wales. When Owain and Hugh Beringar find out about the intentions of Cadwaladr's men they set off in great alarm, only to find that Sister Magdalen, whom we encountered in an earlier existence as the mistress of a Norman Baron, had defended the cell and even captured a high-ranking Welsh youth as a prize. Yet another escape from Norman justice takes place in this novel, and Cadfael is at his most ingenious and devious as he sees his young criminal safely over the border.

Peters's interpretation of history is sharpened by a keen sense of politics. She was always fairly left-wing in her views, but soon became disillusioned with political parties, because "all of them are so flawed, and ultimately let their idealists down" (Pargeter). There is a particular relish in the way she deals with high politics in a novel like *The Holy Thief*. Peters knew first-hand how easily individual liberty could be stifled by a repressive regime as she had been very close to the political situation in Czechoslovaka ever since her first visit in 1947. For many years her distinguished translations of Czech writers and her own regular visits provided a lifeline to the West. One could suggest that her sympathetic understanding of the struggles of the Czech nation to preserve its cultural integrity colors her approach to the heritage of the Welsh beyond her own border in Shropshire.

Many honors were awarded to Edith Pargeter in the last few years of her life, including the Diamond Dagger of the Crime Writers' Association in 1993 and the OBE from the Queen in 1994. Television and radio adaptations of her novels brought her work to an even wider public, throughout the world. But when asked about the reasons for the popularity of her hero she has always been modest in her conclusions:

"I have given up trying to account reasonably for his popularity. Certainly people have told me they find him consoling and reassuring, and look upon him as a personal friend, but I leave it to the individual reader to explain more profoundly." (Pargeter)

The character of Cadfael as he reached old age, and became closer to his son, Olivier, was certainly engrossing Ellis Peters more and more in the later novels. The solution of crimes becomes fairly perfunctory and it was clear that an exploration of the psychology of her elderly monk would have contained many riches had she been able to carry on with the series. What was emerging was an increasingly complex figure, a figure who would always achieve his clearest definition when placed against the challenges represented by the border between England and Wales.

Works Cited

Cam, Helen. *Historical Novels.* London: Historical Association, Pamphlet no. 48, 1961.

Davies, John. *A History of Wales.* English ed. London: Allen Lane, Penguin P, 1993.

Lewis, Margaret. *Edith Pargeter: Ellis Peters.* Bridgend: Seren, 1994.

Pargeter, Edith. Private letter to Margaret Lewis, 28 August 1995.

Peters, Ellis. *Brother Cadfael's Penance.* London: Warner Futura, 1995.

——. *The Holy Thief.* London: Warner Futura, 1993.

——. *A Morbid Taste for Bones.* London: Futura, 1990.

——. *Saint Peter's Fair.* London: Futura, 1991.

——. *The Sanctuary Sparrow.* London: Futura, 1984.

Smith, Goldwin. *A History of England.* 2nd ed. New York: Scribner's, 1957.

Brother Cadfael and His Herbs

Margaret Baker

The inspiration that caused Ellis Peters to make her monk-detective, Brother Cadfael, an herbalist was indeed a stroke of genius, for the good brother's activities, both as healer and as solver of problems, are considerably facilitated by the choice. For one thing, he has his own workshop within the precincts of the abbey. There he can think quietly, conduct private interviews, and, if necessary, hide both objects and people, all impossible within the cloister proper. He also has considerably more opportunity for communication with other people—and thus for gleaning information—than do those whose labors are restricted to the cloister. In addition, he has much more flexibility of movement than do the other monks. Since he administers medicines to those outside the monastery as well as to those within, he has leave to come and go almost at will. His trips to the hospice at Saint Giles and to the inhabitants of the Foregate and the town often serve double duty as sleuthing expeditions and, although he usually asks the abbot in advance if he intends to go anywhere very far or very strange, he frequently pushes that license to the limit or beyond, believing that forgiveness is easier to obtain than permission. Being an herbalist is central to his role as detective.

And Cadfael is definitely a good detective. The question is whether he is also a good herbalist. He is not, interestingly enough, the infirmarer, or doctor, for the monastery; that position belongs to Brother Edmund, although they often work together. Brother Cadfael's job is to supply the medicines. Are those medicines in line with accepted medical practice of the time? Do they have any value today? Investigation shows that most of the remedies Brother Cadfael uses do indeed have at least a reputation for efficacy, and many of them are still in use.

The healing arts of the Middle Ages stemmed from three main sources, all of which Brother Cadfael would have had access to. One source was the traditional herbalism which had been handed down from the ancient Greeks through the Romans and thence to all of the countries of Europe. "Undoubtedly the most influential author in the field of herbals in classical times was Pliny's contemporary, Pedianos Dioskurides, generally known to us today as Dioscorides. . . . Over the years his great work was translated into a variety of languages ranging from Anglo-Saxon and Provencal to Persian and Hebrew (Blunt and Raphael 14). In the usual medieval manner, as well, the translations were retranslated, revised, and reissued until their original was all but lost, and since Dioscorides' work was illustrated, the illustrations were also used again and again, often being distorted beyond recognition in the process. Nevertheless, several Anglo-Saxon versions remain today, arguing a wide circulation in the appropriate time period for Brother Cadfael to have been acquainted with them (Blunt and Raphael 52-53).

In addition to Dioscorides, another popular herbal—this one in Latin—was that of Apuleius Barbarus, or Apuleius Platonicus (Blunt and Raphael 28). As with Dioscorides, both the text and the illustrations of Apuleius' manuscript were reused again and again by authors all over Europe, and several Anglo-Norman copies of this manuscript remain, which could have been available to Cadfael in the twelfth century (Blunt and Raphael 52-53). In fact, since Anglo-Normans were more common in his part of the country than Anglo-Saxons, this might have been an even more likely source than Dioscorides.

None of Peters's books mentions either of these sources by name. In *The Holy Thief,* Cadfael mentions that his remedies are stored in "jars with their Latin inscriptions" (27), which would suggest that he had done some formal studies of the authoritative texts rather than merely having learned from trial and error or from traditional sources. This is supported by his comment in *The Devil's Novice* that "he had also got hold of a copy of Aelfric's list of herbs and trees from the England of a century and a half earlier" (13). No herbal by Aelfric is mentioned in the list of early manuscripts compiled by Tony Hunt (xix-lvi), although certainly the name is well attested. Thus, Peters gives an aura of authority to Brother Cadfael's learning.

She does not, however, discuss the herbs in the standard medieval format, which would have included not only the accepted medical uses, but also the nature of the herbs according to the four humors, as well as the dangers of the herbs and the neutralization of the dangers. For example, a description of rue in a health handbook from the eleventh century tells its nature: "Warm and dry in the third degree," the best type to use: "That which is grown near a fig tree," its usefulness: "It sharpens the eyesight and dissapates [sic] flatulence," its dangers: "It augments the sperm and dampens the desire for coitus," and the neutralization of the dangers: "With foods that multiply the sperm" (Arano, Plate XXXV). These conventions are not followed by Brother Cadfael. In *The Leper of Saint Giles,* he mentions that "alkanet, anemone, mint, figwort, and the grains of oats and barley" are "most of them herbs of Venus and the moon," and that mustard "belongs rather to Mars" (7-8), but this is the only reference in the books to the traditional complex system of classification. Peters must have realized that her modern audience would neither understand the references nor tolerate the plot interruptions necessary for the use of the medieval system.

The second standard source for medieval medicine was the writings and traditions of the great Islamic physicians and scholars. According to Luisa Cogliate Arano, medieval health handbooks—as opposed to mere herbals—originated in the Arabic culture of southern Spain and spread all across Europe (10-17). Although they drew from the herbalist tradition, they also included information concerning the effects of climate, the weather, food, and so forth. Since some of the most famous Arabic physicians were active in Baghdad and Aleppo during the eleventh century, their work would have been available to Cadfael as he traveled "as far afield as Venice, and Cyprus and the Holy Land" while campaigning in the Crusades (*Morbid* 2). Certainly it is evident that he at least learned to use the opium poppy in the Middle East, and not only is poppy syrup his single most prescribed medicine, but he also manages to grow the plants in his English garden, no mean feat, given the difference in climate, and only credible because the period between 1150 and 1300 was exceptionally warm in England, despite the occasional difficult winter. In fact, in *The Pilgrim of Hate,* he specifically mentions the "eastern poppies . . . brought from the Holy Land and reared here with anxious care" (25). His concern extends itself to Brother Mark, his assistant in several of the books, who takes great care to harvest and process the poppy seeds properly (*Saint Peter's* 139). Clearly, Cadfael's experiences in Arabic lands have influenced his medications even as his experiences in tending battle wounds have honed his nursing skills.

The third, and perhaps the most important source of herbal lore was, and is, word of mouth transmission. People tell other people what works for them, what they have heard from their neighbors, what they have read somewhere. Brother Cadfael participates in this tradition as well. When Brother Adam of Reading comes to Shrewsbury to visit, he reveals to Cadfael that he is also an herbalist, and the two spend considerable time discussing the merits of various remedies. Brother Adam finally leaves with his scrip full of seeds and cuttings of Cadfael's most efficacious plants, including the poppies, and promises to return the favor in due time (*Pilgrim* 25). No doubt both men enlarged their knowledge as well as their gardens regularly in that very way.

Nevertheless, the question remains whether the medicines mentioned do indeed have any value. Interestingly enough, that same question, having gone underground for the better part of a century, has now resurfaced, as more and more people, unhappy with standard scientific medical treatment, move towards holistic or homeopathic medicine, including herbal remedies. And now that more information than ever is available to the interested herbalist, it is clear that many of the medicines used by Brother Cadfael truly are useful for his purposes.

Close examination of the books shows that Cadfael is called on to treat a fairly narrow spectrum of complaints. One of the most common of those, predictably, is wounds. This was a violent age, and these are detective novels. Swords and arrows, as well as accidents, abound, often creating serious trauma, and the healer must be ready. Cadfael uses a variety of herbs to treat wounds. Although several of these, such as moneywort, ragwort, adder's tongue, and sanicle, are not commonly listed in modern herbals, others are widely discussed. The plant called "cleavers," for example, used in *The Heretic's Apprentice* in a lotion, "possess [sic] some antibiotic activity" (Mowrey 83), and thus would be useful in treating open sores. Cadfael uses it again in *The Sanctuary Sparrow,* this time mixed with centaury. Again, the cleavers would help the wound, but the centaury is listed now as an aid to digestion, and probably would not have helped a lot.

Another herb that was probably efficacious for wounds is comfrey. Modern authorities concur that "external applications of the leaves are still useful to heal wounds and broken bones" (Weiner 71), but strongly caution against the traditional internal use of comfrey because of potential toxicity. Cadfael's external use is therefore appropriate. Similarly, marshmallow "has been used for hundreds of years as a wound healer. Marshmallow ointments and cremes are used on chapped hands and lips" (Mowrey 33, Tyler 92). Wintergreen's use as an "external analgesic" is well documented (Tyler 147). The active ingredient, methyl salicylate, is related to that in aspirin, and wintergreen, applied as Cadfael does, in lotion form, would ease pain and stimulate healing. Nettle is also "used to heal burns and wounds" (Winer 140), as well as for urinary tract difficulties (Tyler 84), which Cadfael does not treat. In short, many of the remedies which the monk uses to heal the wounded are both appropriate and efficacious.

In addition to wounds, other herbs are used externally for skin conditions and for stings and swelling. Saint John's wort "is . . . commonly applied locally to relieve inflammation and promote healing" (Tyler 124), although it has a more scientific use as an antidepressant (123). It is also "claimed useful in scratches, skin irritations, and insect bites, when mixed with olive oil to form an ointment (Weiner 167), which is the way Cadfael prepares it. In addition, according to Tyler, recent studies indicate possible antiviral properties in the active agents, raising "the possibility that these compounds from Saint John's wort might prove useful in the treatment of AIDS" (Tyler 124). Cadfael also treats bedsores, frost-nipped hands, burns, and skin ulcers. No specific ingredients are given for the salve he rubs into the bedsores, but he says that he uses oil of almonds for the hands because it is a finer type of oil than the hog's fat he usually uses as a base. He applies mulberry leaves to burns—a useful remedy, since they are "rich in grape sugar" and the syrup "has . . . been used as a detergent" (Weiner 136), both of which would tend to retard infection and promote healing. On skin ulcers Cadfael applies both a balm of unspecified ingredients and a paste of mustard. The ingredients might have included the ivy mentioned in *The Leper of Saint Giles,* since "in decoction the leaves have been used to treat skin ulcers and various eruptions" (Weiner 110). One might wonder about the mustard, since it is extremely irritating to the skin, but when "mixed with alcohol, almond oil, or olive oil," it can be used for short periods of time as a "counterirritant" to dilate the blood vessels and thereby increase the blood supply in a certain location (Weiner 138). Cadfael also recognizes that some skin eruptions are due to allergies, and he creates an ointment containing dock and mandrake "for those who got eruptions on their hands or wheezing and sneezing and running eyes during the harvest" (*Pilgrim* 152). Mandrake is best known for the myths and legends which surround it, and is not noted for use with skin eruptions, although it does have a narcotic effect that might alleviate the usual itching and burning of hives (Weiner 124-25). Dock, on the other hand, is commonly used as a treatment for eczema and other skin problems, and would probably be helpful in dealing with allergies (Mowrey 250).

Although treating wounds is urgent and intense, much more of Cadfael's time and efforts are spent dealing with less sensational and more frustrating ailments: colds, with all their attendant miseries. He prescribes a number of different remedies for this universal malady, some of which are still in use today. Horehound, "probably the most effective and pleasant-tasting plant drug," has been used for centuries as an expectorant in cough mixtures and lozenges (Tyler 95). Although its use in over-the-counter medicines was banned in the United States in 1989 by the Federal Drug Administration "because [the FDA] had not received sufficient evidence supporting its efficacy" (Tyler 95), it is still widely used in the British Isles, and "in 1990, the German Commission E approved horehound for the treatment of bronchial catarrh as well as dyspepsia and loss of appetite"

(Tyler 95-96). Often Brother Cadfael combines horehound with other herbs, such as mullein, thyme, rosemary, rue, coltsfoot, mint, and others to treat coughs and sore throats, and each of these also has been shown to be effective. Like horehound, mullein has been approved by the German Commission for use as a remedy for throat irritations and coughs and it "also has some expectorant activity" (Tyler 92). Thyme has "expectorant and antiseptic properties, but functions to relieve bronchospasm as well" (Tyler 96). Flax oil possesses "soothing qualities both internally for coughs and externally for skin irritations" (Weiner 86). Ivy, mentioned for unspecified ailments by Peters, is another expectorant which is commonly used in Europe, although not in the United States (Tyler 97).

Although rue has been "considered beneficial in warding off contagion" it is more commonly used to stimulate abortion than as a cold remedy, and is now considered to be dangerous, particularly if used for an extended period of time (Weiner 166). Surely, Brother Cadfael must have used it in extremely small doses. Opinions differ concerning the use of coltsfoot. Tyler says that "although coltsfoot has useful cough-protective properties, its use cannot be recommended because it also contains toxic . . . alkaloids" (Tyler 91). On the other hand, in Germany it continues to be considered safe in small doses and over a short period of time (Castleman 131). Rosemary is also considered by some to be effective against coughs (Castleman 312-23), but its standard uses are as a digestive aid and a treatment for headaches (Mowrey 225). Since colds are often accompanied by headaches and sick stomachs, Cadfael may have added the rosemary in order to combat these secondary problems. Mint—particularly peppermint—is also considered an effective digestive aid, although not a decongestant or expectorant. However, mint, along with honey, is widely used as a flavoring agent to disguise the bitterness or unpleasant taste of other medications, and may have been used in this way in Cadfael's cough mixture. Mustard is also used both in the cough mixture and as a chest rub or plaster for colds and coughs, both widely honored traditional remedies. Many of the cough syrups also include a few drops of poppy syrup, no doubt to ease pain and induce sleep, parallel to the modern use of codeine. And often Cadfael mixes all the ingredients into wine, probably for the same reason, although his stipulation in *Monk's-Hood* of red cherry wine is interesting, since wild cherry bark is noted for its effectiveness "as an expectorant and mild sedative" (Castleman 372). Whether the wine would also contain these properties is, of course, not known. At any rate, it is clear that Ellis Peters understood the use of a number of the major herbal cough and sore throat remedies when she put them into Brother Cadfael's medicine chest.

Although the principal afflictions that Cadfael knows and treats are wounds and respiratory problems, they are by no means the only ones, and some of the others are quite unusual, either from the standpoint of the ailment or of the medicine. Readers of *The Confession of Brother Haluin* might find it a little strange that a monk should know that hyssop induces abortion, even when others are responsible for the procedure (19). However, Cadfael lived much of his life outside the monastery, and he also understands human nature; no doubt he knows much that he does not need to use. Similarly, it might seem odd that a man who has never raised a family should be an expert in baby colic, but in *The Raven in the Foregate* he undertakes to treat that malady with a combination of ingredients that probably seemed appropriate to him, but which would horrify many today. The mixture includes "dill, fennel, mint, just a morsel of poppy juice . . . and honey to make it agreeable to the taste" (*Raven* 112). Gwilt points out that "infant colic was (and is) treated with a cordial containing dill . . . and/or fennel . . . flavoured with mint as a carminative" (808). According to Castleman, "research supports dill's 3,000 years of use as a digestive aid" (148) and he goes on to note that "it helps prevent the formation of intestinal gas bubbles." Fennel is also used for intestinal gas, "and especially to prevent colic in babies" (Weiner 85). Peppermint oil is widely recognized as a digestive aid (Tyler 56). However, the thought of giving an opiate, no matter how weak the solution, to a month-old baby is counter to modern wisdom. And in recent years, mothers of infants and young children have been expressly warned against giving them honey because of the danger of infant botulism which it sometimes carries. Perhaps because Peters never had any children of her own, Brother Cadfael seems to have involved himself in something that he didn't know enough about when he deals with baby colic.

Interesting as well are the remedies he uses for "fits" or "swoons." When the grandmother in *The Sanctuary Sparrow* suffers a fit and falls down the stairs, he gives her a powder of rare oak mistletoe (26). Although many avoid mistletoe entirely because of its toxicity, its reputation in traditional herbalism is as a treatment for high blood pressure (Tyler 180, Castleman 259). Certainly an old woman already being treated for a heart condition would benefit from any lowering of her blood pressure. On the other hand, a young woman who swoons in *The Leper of Saint Giles* is revived with mint and sorrel vinegar combined with bitter herbs into a mixture used as smelling salts (89). If the mixture contained the strong essential oil of peppermint rather than the milder fragrance of the leaves, that combination would make a very powerful scent indeed and no doubt was an effective remedy. Since many of these novels are romances as well as detective stories, they often feature young women with heartaches. One such is sent to her bed by Brother Cadfael carrying a little pillow containing lavender, which he says is good for the heart and spirit and will help her to sleep (*Rare* 56). He has, as usual, prescribed appropriately, since Weiner says that lavender is "an aromatic stimulant . . . and tonic, to treat nervous languor and headache" (116). Oats may seem to be another oddity as a medicine, especially as an ingredient in non-specific salves and lotions. Any parent who has had to deal with children uncomfortable with chickenpox, however, has reason to know that finely ground oatmeal, made into a lotion or dissolved in bath water, can relieve itching for an appreciable period of time. No doubt the early herbalists knew this as well.

One of Cadfael's major skills lies in the management of pain. In these books, the most frequently mentioned medication by far is the syrup the good brother makes from eastern poppies. In an age when pain was an ever-present problem, the poppy syrup must have seemed almost miraculous, and Brother Cadfael uses it often, both alone and in conjunction with other herbs. He gives it to the wounded, to the terminally ill, even to a baby. He uses it to lull the aged and suffering to sleep, knowing that sleep is also a healer. He uses it to calm troubled souls and give them the courage to face their problems. He never worries about addiction or about improper use, knowing that he is the only source and can regulate the consumption.

However, poppy syrup is not the only pain reliever available to Cadfael. Woundwort is also administered, along with Saint John's wort, for pain and to promote healing. Woundwort is not listed in modern herbals, apparently because it is not a specific herb, but refers to a group of similar plants with different effects. However, Saint John's wort does help relieve inflammation, as has been pointed out. Hemlock is also used to alleviate pain in *The Potter's Field,* although not by Brother Cadfael. Since hemlock has been known as a deadly poison since ancient times, he understands that its use as a pain reliever is not appropriate. In fact, he reminds Donata that hemlock is "used against pain when other things fail, but in this strength it would end pain forever" (172). She, however, has a different reason for using hemlock, and she keeps it close beside her.

Hemlock is not the only poison to be found in these books, either. In fact, the whole plot of *Monk's-Hood* turns on the fact that the plant variously called monk's hood or wolfsbane "and all its relatives are swift and fatal poisons" (40). Nevertheless, Cadfael uses it, with due care, as a rub for the aching limbs of the elderly brothers who can no longer leave their beds, and "used externally as a liniment, the plant has proved useful in the treatment of neuralgic and rheumatic pains" (Weiner 203). When the liniment is used to poison a tenant of one of the abbey's houses, Cadfael tries to get the man to swallow mustard, milk, and egg. The attempted remedies are appropriate, since mustard is a powerful emetic, and milk and egg are routinely administered to soothe and coat the linings of the digestive tract and to neutralize the effects of poisonous substances.

Other herbs are mentioned in the books. Alkanet, anemone, angelica, borage and broom, all have a place in the dispensary of the modern herbalist as well as in that of Brother Cadfael, although the specific ways in which he applies them are not clearly stated. However, one more point must be made about his medieval medicine, and that is that he knows the importance of the bedside manner. Over and over, as remedies are mentioned and administered, they are accompanied with heated rocks to warm a bed for a chilled patient, with constant attendance by those willing to nurse aching bodies and spirits, with nourishing food and calming drinks. And when Cadfael realizes that his remedies can no longer be effective, he calls in the priest to ease the soul, administers poppy syrup to ease the body, and, without heroic measures, allows the inevitable to happen. Modern medicine could probably take a lesson.

According to Margaret Lewis, Edith Pargeter spent seven years working as an assistant in a chemist's shop or drug store while she began her writing career. "Much of her knowledge of medicinal drugs came from this time" (13). Obviously, she learned her lessons well and passed those lessons on to her character, Brother Cadfael. Not only does he always solve the crime, but he initiates his associates—and the modern reader—into the mysteries of herbal healing.

Works Cited

Arano, Luisa Cogliate. *The Medieval Health Handbook: Tacuinum Sanitatis.* New York: George Braziller, 1976.

Blunt, Wilfrid, and Sandra Raphael. *The Illustrated Herbal.* New York: Thames and Hudson, 1979.

Castleman, Michael. *The Healing Herbs: The Ultimate Guide to the Curative Power of Nature's Medicine.* Emmaus, PA: Rodale, 1991.

Gwilt, J. R. "Brother Cadfael's Herbiary." *The Pharmaceutical Journal* December 19/26 (1992): 807-09.

Hunt, Tony. *Plant Names of Medieval England.* Cambridge: Brewer, 1989.

Lewis, Margaret. *Edith Pargeter: Ellis Peters.* Bridgend: Seren, 1994.

Mowrey, Daniel B. *The Scientific Validation of Herbal Medicine.* New Canaan, CT: Keats, 1986.

Peters, Ellis. *The Confession of Brother Haluin.* New York: Mysterious P, 1988.

——. *The Devil's Novice.* New York: Mysterious P, 1984.

——. *The Holy Thief.* New York: Mysterious P, 1992.

——. *The Leper of Saint Giles.* New York: Mysterious P, 1981.

——. *Monk's-Hood.* New York: Mysterious P, 1980.

——. *A Morbid Taste for Bones.* New York: Mysterious P, 1977.

——. *The Pilgrim of Hate.* New York: Morrow, 1984.

——. *The Potter's Field.* New York: Mysterious P, 1990.

——. *A Rare Benedictine.* New York: Mysterious P, 1989.

——. *The Raven in the Foregate.* New York: Fawcett Crest, 1986.

——. *Saint Peter's Fair.* New York: Fawcett Crest, 1981.

——. *The Sanctuary Sparrow.* New York: Morrow, 1983.

Tyler, Varro E. *Herbs of Choice: The Therapeutic Use of Phytomedicinals.* New York: Pharmaceutical Products, 1994.

Weiner, Michael A. *Weiner's Herbal: The Guide to Herb Medicine.* New York: Stein and Day, 1980.

Vision in *A Rare Benedictine*

Carol A. Mylod

Unique in Ellis Peters's twenty-one-book Brother Cadfael mystery series because it is a collection of three short stories rather than a novel, *A Rare Benedictine* delights in many ways— from the color illustrations that evoke the mysterious and symbolic nature of Byzantine art with its mask-like faces and daunting lack of perspective to the stories themselves that unfold over a twenty-year period in Cadfael's life (AD 1120 to 1140) and are masterfully tied together by the author's play on images of light and dark or vision and blindness.

Considering that the stories were initially published at different times over a six-year period, it is remarkable how well their central images coalesce. The titles of the stories point the way to understanding their meaning: "The Light on the Road to Woodstock," "The Price of Light," and "Eye Witness." In addition to aspects of physical blindness on the part of the characters, their moral blindness is intertwined with those staples of medieval literature, the seven deadly sins. The exploration of those tantalizing sins is, perhaps, more overt in *A Rare Benedictine* than it is in the novels of the series.

Readers particularly appreciate the stories in *A Rare Benedictine* because of the "light" they shed on Brother Cadfael's early life, his character, and his vocation. Peters wrote in a brief introduction that her benevolent detective, Brother Cadfael, a man possessed of "wide worldly experience and an inexhaustible fund of resigned tolerance for the human condition," acts as "an agent of justice in the centre of the action" (4-5).

Some readers might compare Cadfael's volte-face at age forty, from man-at-arms to monk, to the Biblical account of Saint Paul's conversion on the road to Damascus where he saw a light from Heaven, heard the voice of God, and was struck blind for three days until he was baptized by Ananias. The Acts of the Apostles comment about Paul: "And straightway there fell from his eyes something like scales and he recovered his sight, and arose and was baptized" (9:18).

Contradicting this viewpoint, Peters insisted in her introduction that what happened to Cadfael on the road to Woodstock was not a conversion "but simply the acceptance of a revelation from within that the life he had lived to date, active, mobile and often violent, had reached its natural end" (*Rare* 7). In other Chronicles, Cadfael seems to attribute to the hand of God a more active role in his decision to become a Benedictine lay brother. For example, in *The Potter's Field,* Cadfael muses about the turning point in his life and describes it as a "revelation of God" and as "emergence into light" (9). He recalls:

After all manner of journeyings, fighting, endurance, the sudden irresistible longing to turn about and withdraw into quietness, remained a mystery. Not a retreat, certainly. Rather an emergence into light and certainty. He never could explain it or describe it. All he could say was that he had a revelation of God, and had turned where he was pointed, and come where he was called. (*Potter's* 9)

In "A Light on the Road to Woodstock," with years of exciting adventures behind him, Cadfael wonders what lies ahead: "There was no identifiable light beckoning him anywhere along the road. The road was wide, fair and full of savor, but without signposts" (*Rare* 15). Cadfael's future was hidden from him but he knew "it must be something new and momentous, a door opening into another room" (*Rare* 19).

In the course of the story, Cadfael saves the life of his master, Roger Mauduit, when Lady Mauduit's lover, Goscelin, attempts to murder him on a dark and moonless night in the dense forest of Woodstock. Cadfael also rescues Prior Heribert from the darkness of a hay-store where Roger had imprisoned him.

At the end of the story, Cadfael is drawn by the dim light of Vespers in the parish church and invited by a young acolyte with eyes "as solemn as ever was angelic messenger" to lay aside his weapons (*Rare* 50). Cadfael tells Prior Heribert that he is at the turning of his life and asks to accompany him to the Abbey of Saint Peter and Saint Paul in Shrewsbury. The literal darkness of the setting has flowed into the figurative meaning of light as knowledge, understanding, and grace. This progression occurs again and again in these engrossing short stories.

In "The Price of Light," the repellent, aging, and morally blind Lord Hamo FitzHamon, fearing for his soul's salvation, donates to the Abbey two valuable silver candlesticks as well as the rent from one of his tenant farms to supply light for Our Lady's altar throughout the year. When Brother Oswald, the almoner, suggests that the worth of the candlesticks could feed his poor petitioners throughout the winter, that sycophantic toady, Brother Jerome, comments: "Could any price be too high for the lighting of this holy altar?" (*Rare* 96). When the villein Elfgiva clandestinely removes the candlesticks from the altar, old, frail, almost blindBrother Jordan believes that he sees the Blessed Virgin herself making her will known about the disposition of the candlesticks.

The title of the third story, "Eye Witness," carries the most ironic connotation. Jacob of Bouldon steals the rent collection from the Abbey's chief steward, William Rede, and attempts his murder. Jacob betrays himself when he makes a second attempt at murder, erroneously believing that the old Welsh beggar, Rhodri Fychan, blind from birth, had a possible vantage point to view the first crime. Jacob cursed when he saw Rhodri: "For in the wrinkled, lively face the lantern showed two eyes that caught reflected light though they had none of their own, eyes as opaque as gray pebbles and as insensitive" (*Rare* 146). The money Jacob stole was found and returned by the honest trader, Warin Harefoot, who had kept his "eye" on Jacob (*Rare* 149).

Brother Eutropius, another character in the story, experiences moral vision "like a thunderbolt of revelation" regarding his contemplated but rejected act of suicide (*Rare* 109). Just as he is about to throw himself into the river Severn, Madog of the Dead Boat finds the unconscious William Rede and cries "Drowned Man!" For Brother Eutropius, "it was as if God himself had set before him, like a lightning stroke from heaven, the enormity of the act he contemplated" (*Rare* 138).

Interestingly enough, the most morally corrupt character in the book is not either of the two men who attempts murder, i.e., Goscelin in "A Light on the Road to Woodstock" and Jacob of Bouldon in "Eye Witness," but is, rather, Lord Hamo FitzHamon in "The Price of Light." One sentence says it all about Hamo's gluttony, lust, anger, and pride. The conniving and dishonorable Hamo who had probably worn out more than one wife was "a gross feeder, a heavy drinker, a self-indulgent lecher, a harsh landlord and a brutal master" (*Rare* 57).

As a counterweight to the corrupt characters, admirable characters abound in these stories, notably Prior Heribert in "A Light on the Road to Woodstock" who demonstrates personal bravery as well as steadfast devotion to duty, and Eddi Rede in "Eye Witness" who risks his life in catching the man who tried to murder his father. Eddi is eager to be the bait in the trap when Cadfael tells him that "whoever fears an eye witness shall have but this one night to act" (*Rare* 136).

The most ideal characters in the book are the villeins Elfgiva and Alard from "The Price of Light" who exhibit selfless love, fidelity, courage, and, above all, unobtrusive charity—in contrast to Hamo's showy, calculating charity. By selling the silver candlesticks that, by rights, belonged to Alard who had made them, and by giving all the gold coins realized from the sale to the church in order to feed the poor, they gave everything they possessed in gratitude to God for being free from villeinage and for finding each other again after Alard's flight from Hamo. The lily that inspired the shape of Alard's candlesticks is paradoxically a symbol for both life and death. The use of this symbol may be a commentary on the diametrically opposed moral lives of the two men who claim ownership of the candlesticks, Alard and Hamo.

Elfgiva tells Cadfael that if Alard is of the same mind: "I have made a vow to Our Lady, who leant me her semblance in the old man's eyes, that we will sell these candlesticks where they may fetch their proper price, and that price shall be delivered to your almoner to feed the hungry. And that will be our gift, Alard's and mine, though no one will ever know" (*Rare* 89).

Epiphanies, large and small, abound in these beautifully crafted short stories. The characters' eyes are opened in so many different ways. Roger Mauduit ruefully realizes that his wife has taken a lover while he was away in Normandy, and they want him dead in order to inherit his property. The querulous and argumentative William Rede, constantly at loggerheads with his "brawler" and "gamester" (*Rare* 105) son, Eddi, has an insight into the deep, abiding love that exists between them.

The aging Lord Hamo begins to realize his mortality. His wife, Lady Hamo, sees that her affair with a young groom is ill-concealed from the sharp eyes of Brother Cadfael and, possibly, from other keen observers. Elfgiva and Alard appreciate the value of love, happiness, and freedom, "for what was gold, what was silver by comparison?" (*Rare* 97). Cadfael is enlightened with the direction his future is going to take. He will love and serve God by loving and serving his fellow man as a Benedictine lay brother.

Although a minor character in *A Rare Benedictine*, Brother Eutropius and his story exemplify one of the major themes in all of Ellis Peters's writing. The worst thing that a person can do in an Ellis Peters story is not to commit a mortal sin like murder (murderers are sometimes portrayed as sympathetic characters if they repent and atone, e.g., Meurig in *Monk's-Hood* or Eluid ap Griffith in *Dead Man's Ransom*) but, rather, to die unshriven after committing a mortal sin as Adam Courcelle does in *One Corpse Too Many*.

Fearing that the unrepentant murderer, Adam Courcelle, who is killed in single combat will be denied eternal salvation, Cadfael comments that "every untimely death, every man cut down in his vigor and strength without time for repentance and reparation, is one corpse too many" (*Rare* 188). In contrast to Adam Courcelle, Eutropius recognizes the enormity of the sin of despair that led to his attempted suicide, and he is quickly "penitent," "confessed," and "absolved" of his mortal sin (138-39).

With his keen insight into the human condition and his great faith, Cadfael knew that some day "a sudden irresistible motion of grace" would pierce Eutropius's "carapace," but Cadfael was not in a hurry "where souls were concerned. There was plenty of elbow room in eternity" (*Rare* 111).

Deeply and artfully embedded in these three lively detective stories with vivid characterizations, wonderfully accurate historical settings, and intricate mysteries are mini-parables on the virtues of faith, hope, and charity, and thoughtful explorations of fidelity, chastity, loyalty, bravery, honor, and sacrifice. Surely the moral vision of Ellis Peters as exemplified by her Brother Cadfael series is one very important source of the great appeal of the stories.

Works Cited

Peters, Ellis. *One Corpse Too Many*. New York: Ballantine, 1979.
——. *The Potter's Field*. New York: Mysterious, 1990.
——. *A Rare Benedictine*. New York: Mysterious, 1988.

Contributors

Margaret P. Baker teaches English at Brigham Young University-Hawaii. She is a long-time reader of mystery novels and a recent lover of gardening and enjoyed combining those two interests in examining Brother Cadfael's herbs.

Anthony Hopkins teaches English and Humanities at Glendon College, York University, Toronto. His publications include *An Outline of the Plays of Edward Albee* and *Songs from the Front and Rear: Canadian Servicemen's Songs of the Second World War*.

Judith Kollmann is professor of English at the University of Michigan-Flint. Her area of specialization is medieval literature, although she has several areas of scholarly interest. Her publications include a forthcoming *Reader's Guide to John Varley*, "The Centaur" in *Mythical and Fabulous Creatures: A Source Book and Research Guide,* ed. Malcolm South, "*Grendel* and the Tarot," in *Spectrum of the Fantastic,* ed. Donald Palumbo, and numerous articles on Charles Williams. She is currently engaged in editing an encyclopedia on Charles Williams.

Margaret Lewis is the authorized biographer of mystery writer Ngaio Marsh (*Ngaio Marsh: A Life,* Chatto and Windus, 1991) and wrote *Edith Pargeter: Ellis Peters* for the Seren Press Borderlines Series in 1994. Born in Northern Ireland, and educated in Canada, Dr. Lewis now lives in the north of England with her family.

Kayla McKinney Wiggins is a professor of literature, speech, and drama at Martin Methodist College in Pulaski, Tennessee. Her research interests include modern drama, popular fiction, and folklore in literature. Her recent research focuses primarily on the influence of Celtic matter on modern and contemporary literature. Professor Wiggins is the author of *Modern Verse Drama in English* (Greenwood, 1993) and a contributing author to *John Arden and Margaretta D'Arcy: A Casebook* (Garland, 1995).

Carol Mylod is an adjunct assistant professor of English at Molloy College, Rockville Centre, New York. She holds a Masters in History as well as Masters and Doctor of Arts Degrees in English from St. John's University. After starting her working life by teaching history to high school students in Athens, Greece, and, later, in New York City, she switched in mid-career to teaching English at Adelphi University and St. John's University. As a member of the Association of Municipal Historians of New York State, Mylod has authored a variety of articles on local history.

Marcia J. Songer is assistant chair of the English Department at East Tennessee State University, where she teaches English as a Second Language, literature of Western civilization, and African literature. Long a participant in the Detective and Mystery Fiction area of the Popular Culture Association, she has given several conference papers on Brother Cadfael.

Anita M. Vickers is assistant professor of Humanities and English at The Pennsylvania State University where she teaches courses in American literature, women's studies, and specialized writing courses. She has published articles and presented conference papers in these areas.